Tou
(The Touch Series, #2)
By t.h. snyder

Heather,
thanks for your support!

© 2013 t. h. snyder (Tiffany Snyder)

Published by t. h. snyder

First published in 2013. All rights reserved. This book is copyright. Apart from the fair purpose of private study, research or review as permitted by the Copyright Act, no part may be reproduced without written permission.

This book is licensed for your personal enjoyment only. This book may not be re-sold or given away to other people. If you would like to share this book with another person, please purchase an additional copy for each recipient. If you're reading this book and did not purchase it, or it was not purchased for your use only, then please return and purchase your own copy. Thank you for respecting the hard work of this author.

This is a work of fiction. Names, characters, places, and incidents are the product of the imagination or are used fictitiously. Any resemblance to actual, locales or persons, living or dead, is entirely coincidental.

Images Copyright http://www.selfpubbookcovers.com/

Acknowledgements

This entire journey has been a dream come true and I couldn't have done it without all of you.

I appreciate all the support of my fans on Facebook, Twitter, Goodreads and Instagram…it's because of you I continue to write every day.

My family! You are amazing and always encourage me to do what I believe in, no matter who says otherwise. I love you Mom, Angie, Mar and Dad!!

The two most important people in my life, my kids Raeghyn and Mason. I love you more than you will ever know…to infinity and beyond.

My reading partner in crime Trisha. Regardless of our busy schedules you always find the time to fit me in…somewhere.

My amazing beta girls! Thank you for taking the time out of your busy lives to read my book. You all mean the world to me….love you STAR BETA SQUAD Jenn, Tabitha, Susan, Crystal, Sandee, Barbara, Amelia, Pam, and Jennifer.

Special author shout out to Margaret McHeyzer for guiding me under her wings. I love you for never giving up on me and giving me a good slap when I need it.

Prologue
Summer 2013

Someone once told me everyone has a special someone they are meant to be with forever. A man who will be my world, my partner in life, and the one person I can grow old with and always be by my side.

Maybe I never found that right person to begin with.

No! That can't be right. I had my person and I was too wrapped up in my own little bubble to realize what was right in front of me.

He was the one.

He was my forever.

I screwed it up over my own damn selfish needs.

I thought I had chosen the path in life that was best for me, but I seem to have lost my soul mate along the way.

Waiting to board a plane back to Boston, I sit here wondering if I made the right choices in life. Did I follow the path that would take me in the right direction? Could I have done something different that would change the outcomes I'm faced with right now?

I haven't seen or spoken to him in four months. Four long, torturous months dealing with what I did to us and our happily ever after. I know I'll run into him soon, but when I do I'm not sure how he'll react. He could accept me in an embrace or turn the corner and run the other way.

What did I do?

The choices I've made changed my life in only a short period of time and I fear I may have lost him forever.

At one time he was all I ever knew. The two of us were so in sync with the other no force field could tear us apart. I can hear him whisper in my ear. "Chloe you and I will stand the test of time because I was touched by you and only you."

I, Chloe Taylor, am faced with a decision I may not like myself for in the next few hours. Only time will tell what is meant to be and for now I have a much bigger weight on my plate than that of my love life.

Part One
How We Became an Us

Chapter 1
August 2005

CHLOE

I sit under the giant weeping willow tree at my parent's house, waiting for him. This is our meeting spot, the place where we can be together and no one can bother us. We've been meeting up at this exact tree for years and now it's the last time he'll come and meet me as my high school boyfriend.

I'm leaving for college tomorrow.

I'll be moving to New York to attend NYU with a few friends and my cousin Lucy. This is a huge opportunity for me. I'm more than ecstatic to start a new chapter of my life, only if the distance from my boyfriend wasn't making me have second thoughts.

Derrick and I have known each other since the first grade when his family moved to Boston. Since that time we've always been friends, but we never shared our true feelings for one another until our junior year of high school.

I sit back on the bench under our tree and remember like it was yesterday.

It was the day before our junior prom when I had my very first emotional melt down in front of Derrick.

I was asked by quite a few of my classmates to go to prom, but I kept saying no in hopes that Derrick would ask me.

It's the day before prom and I sit in my room crying for hours.

How is it possible that Chloe Taylor is going to miss prom because of a guy?

Derrick climbs up to my bedroom window and asks me what's wrong. I'm so upset, so embarrassed. I don't think I can pull up the courage to tell him that he's the reason I'm having an emotional breakdown.

"Chloe what's wrong, why are you crying?" He asks.

"It's nothing I can talk to you about Derrick." I reply in between sniffles.

"Come on Chloe, you know you can talk to me about anything. We're damn good friends and I won't judge you if that's what you're worried about." He tells me in his Dr. Phil voice.

I let out a giggle. Derrick always knows how to make me laugh when I'm sad. He's been here for me for years and I'm always too afraid to tell him how I feel. My god, what if he doesn't feel the same way about me. Could I deal with the rejection of Derrick Peters? I'm the most popular girl in my school and here I am swooning over a guy that may not like me more than just a friend.

"It's just...ugh...god Derrick it's so embarrassing." I tell him with my hands hiding my face.

"Look, I'm not going to ask you again so if you want to tell me fine. If not then I'll just climb back out of your room and leave you be." He says in a pissed off tone.

"No please don't go Derrick. I'm sorry for being all girly with you. I'm just really upset that I don't have a date to prom tomorrow."

I remove my hands from my face and look up into his baby blue eyes. He's hysterically laughing at me. What the hell is wrong with this guy and why do I find myself so attracted by the fact that he's making fun of me?

"Whatever asshole, this is exactly why I wasn't going to say anything to you." *I respond to him and begin to stand moving across my bedroom.*

"Stop it Chloe. I'm not laughing at you. I just find it odd that over a dozen guys asked you to prom and yet you still don't have a date. Why is that Chloe?" *He asks while he walks over to me and begins staring at my lips.*

I look up into his eyes and see my friend, but as I begin to look a little deeper I see something I never noticed before. I see his desire for me.

"I guess I was just waiting for the right guy to ask me." *I say biting my thumb nail in a nervous gesture.*

He's looking down at me intently and I can tell the wheels are spinning in his head.

"Well if you had someone in mind why didn't you just ask him?"

I let out a laugh.

"Oh come on Derrick that's just not right. This is prom and it's customary for the gentleman to ask the lady." *I tell him.*

"Well the way I see it, if you would've broken the custom and just asked the guy you wanted to go with you wouldn't be in this predicament. Now would you?" *He asks moving closer to me.*

I begin to feel nervous, anxious that Derrick Peters is coming so close to me. I'm not sure what he's up to, but with the look in his eyes I can tell that any friendship I share with him is about to be thrown out the window.

"Derrick?" I ask in a whisper.

"Yes Chloe." He replies

He's so close to me in this moment. I can feel his warm breath and the hairs on the back of my neck start to stand. I know that I'm attracted to this guy, but I have no idea what game he's playing with me.

"I was wondering." I tell him.

"Wondering what Chloe?" He asks.

He is seriously standing only inches from me. I can feel the heat of his chest radiating onto me. I want to grab hold of his polo and pull his body against my own.

"Umm Derrick, do you have plans for tomorrow night?" I ask closing my eyes.

I want him to kiss me more than anything. I've never wanted anything more in my entire life. I can smell the spearmint gum in his mouth. I can't stop the feelings my body is craving for this guy to touch me.

"Actually yes Chloe, I do." He replies. "I plan on taking the most beautiful girl to the prom and having the time of our lives."

"Oh!" I say with a pout, still keeping my eyes closed.

I can feel his arm lift to his side and in a matter of seconds his fingers on my face pulling me in closer to him.

He leans down to me and puts his lips against mine. For a moment I feel that this act is foreign to us, but within a few seconds I'm opening my lips to welcome a deeper kiss.

This is the moment I've been waiting for way too long. I've been crushing on Derrick for years and now I'm finally sharing a moment with him that could change everything between us.

I'm so involved in my own brain that I realize I'm not enjoying the fact that his mouth is intertwined with my own. I feel his tongue against mine and his hands begin to roam from the sides of my face down my neck and along the length of my torso. For so long I imagined what this moment would be like and here we are together at last. Slowly Derrick starts to pull away and rather than move from me he pulls me tightly into his embrace. I can feel his heart beating a mile a minute through our clothes.

"Chloe, I couldn't stand to wait another minute to kiss you." He says almost breathless.

"Derrick you have nothing to worry about. I've wanted you to do that forever." I reply with a giggle.

"Good! So now nothing will be weird when I let you go?" He asks.

"Nothing has or will ever be weird with us Derrick. Now that I've been touched by you things will never be the same." I told him standing up on my tip toes to get another kiss.

The sound of the weeping willow branches moving pulls me out of my daydream and I can smell the heavenly scent that is Derrick. I look over in his direction and see him walking toward me. He really is quite handsome in his polo and khaki shorts. His light brown hair is styled just perfect and his gorgeous baby blue eyes are looking right at me.

He sits down next to me and wipes tears from my cheeks. I hadn't realized I had been crying.

I really am going to miss being so close to him.

DERRICK

I've been running around like a chicken with my head cut off for the past few weeks. Not only do I need to prepare to move to Cambridge, but my girlfriend is moving away to New York. Why the fuck does Chloe have to go find herself hundreds of miles away from here? Seriously, what does NYU have that Harvard doesn't?

I continue to go through my room to make sure I've packed up all the things I need for the dorms. I come across a picture of me and Chloe from junior prom. My heart begins to beat a mile a minute as I remember our prom, our first dance and the night she became my girlfriend.

Chloe and I were drawn to one another from the first moment we met, well at least I was, but things didn't really start up until the end of our junior year. Since then we've been pretty much inseparable

I've had a crush on this girl for years, but was always standing along the sidelines of all the other jocks waiting to ask her out. Don't get me wrong, I had my own line-up waiting for me, but Chloe was the one that always seemed to catch my eye.

It's the night of prom. I'm on my way to her house to pick her up in my car. I feel like an ass for not having something fancier to take her to prom, but we did plan this kind of last minute.

I walk toward her house and can feel the butterflies creeping up as I knock on her front door. I am met with her parents and sister, who fortunately have liked me from the start.

Bryce gives me the usual lecture and curfew guidelines while Teresa and Char set us up out by our tree for pictures.

Everything is perfect.

We meet up with a few of our friends to take pictures and talk about after prom parties.

I hold Chloe in my arms for most of the time. We dance the night away and just embrace every moment of being together.

I come back to the land of the living and out of my trance. I smile to myself. We really did have the time of our lives that night.

Chloe is the one person I know I cannot live without. I really don't know how we're going to make it through our first year of college without one another. But I'm damned well going to try just about anything to keep Chloe as my girl.

I finish up a few last minute things at my house and get ready to go meet Chloe for our date. I stop at the flower shop down the block and grab a bouquet of flowers that I know she'll love. I also make a point to pack us a picnic basket with all of her favorite foods from town. I figure I might as well show her all the great things she'll be missing by leaving Boston.

I pull into her parents' driveway and see that both Bryce and Teresa are sitting out on the front porch. I hop out of my car, grab the stuff out of the backseat and send a wave in their direction. Making my way over to our spot I'm flooded with so many memories we shared in this exact spot. I go around to the back side of the weeping willow tree so that she doesn't see me coming through the branches. I can see that she's sitting on the bench and her knees are pulled up against her chest. She's wearing a light pink sundress and her long, dark waves are casting a curtain over her shoulders.

I love this girl.

She looks to be deep in thought I hate to interrupt any memories she's thinking back on in this moment. This transition is going to be hard on both of us, but there's nothing that can break what the two of us share.

I set down the things I brought for our picnic and walk over to the bench. She can sense that I'm coming and she shifts her body to look over in my direction. As her face looks up to mine I can see that she's been crying and her big brown eyes are now red and puffy with sadness.

I quickly sit down on our bench next to her and pull her into my lap. I stroke the soft hair down her back and pull her face to look at me.

"What has my girl so sad?" I ask while kissing her lightly on her lips.

"I'm leaving tomorrow Derrick and this is the last time we'll be in this special spot together." She says while sobbing.

"Oh Chloe, as much as I hate this too, we'll make it work. I promise."

I pull back her thick hair so that I can see her beautiful face. I wipe away the tears that are running down her cheeks and kiss her on each side of her face. She gives me a smile that I know speaks a hundred words. She is mine forever.

"I have a great afternoon planned for us, so how about you shake off this feeling you have and let's go have some fun together."

"You really are the best Derrick Peters. I'm going to miss you so much."

She stands up off of my lap and pulls me up with her. I grab her back in my arms and twirl her under our tree.

This will forever be our place, no matter how many miles apart we may be.

"So what's the plan for today?" She asks.

"Well I have a picnic basket and all of your favorites inside. I also brought you some flowers." I hand her the bouquet and kiss her gently on her forehead.

She takes a whiff of their sweet scent and grabs my hand into her own.

"Where would you like to take our picnic?

"I would love for us to spend the entire afternoon under our tree. This is our getaway place, so why not just spend our time hidden under the branches?"

"I think that's a perfect idea. After we're done eating how about we go for a swim and then I have a little going away present for you." She remarks with a coy smirk.

"I'm all for it!" I tell her while getting out the blanket and setting up our lunch.

We share our picnic foods and reminisce about all the times we've shared together. We laugh over the awkward moments, the heartbreaks we caused once everyone knew we were together, the parties with our friends and what our futures hold after college.

After our time under the tree I'm confident knowing that my girl loves me and will miss me as much as I will her. She's my world and no matter what we'll make it through anything life throws our way.

Chapter 2

CHLOE

Derrick has made our last day together absolutely perfect. He wasn't joking when he said he packed all of my favorite things, but the one I'll miss the most is him. We plan to come home as often as possible so that we can be together, but with his football schedule and classes it's going to be tough.

I'm the type of person that needs routine and schedules in my life, without them I go crazy. It will be my mission to get on track as quickly as possible so that I can plan as many visits as I can to Cambridge. I've never missed watching Derrick play a game…for anything, even when we were just friends. He says I'm his lucky charm. I hope his winning streak doesn't dry up because I won't be around to see him play.

I'm wrapped up in his arms on our bench and I can feel myself beginning to doze off. Derrick runs his fingertips up and down my arms and a chill ignites thousands of goose bumps across my body. This man has a way with his fingers and with just a mere touch he can have me all girl crazy. I love him and will never…ever let him go.

He leans me slightly forward from his body and pulls all my dark brown hair to the side so that my neck is completely bare to the left. I scoot in closer to him and rest my back against his firm chest. I feel so content with him. I really don't want this day to end.

He leans forward and nips at my ear while placing light kisses along my jaw leading down to my neck. This is my most sensitive spot and he knows it all too well.

"Excuse me Derrick, what do you think you're doing?" I ask with a giggle.

"Well I guess I'm doing something wrong here if you have to ask me what the hell I'm doing."

"Ah come on babe, I was just joking. I love when you kiss me like that. It sends chills through my body."

"Yes, that was my intent and I also plan to have that body doing something else really soon."

He turns and lifts me so that I'm straddling his hips and I can look directly in his eyes. Those baby blues are god damn amazing and he can say so much just by looking at me. I lean into him and wrap my arms around his neck.

"I love you Derrick and I'll never forget moments like this with you."

I kiss him hard and with such intensity. I don't know how soon I'll be with him again. He must feel the anxiety coming from me because he kisses me back with such fierceness.

He nips my lips and slides his tongue in my mouth. We've kissed a million times before, but nothing as passionate as this.

"I love you so much Chloe and I'll never give you up. Do you hear me? You are mine and will be forever. Whatever we have to do to keep our love alive, we will."

Tears begin to prick my eyelids as we continue to kiss and I want to believe that we'll make it through the next year as a couple.

"Chloe, I really can't wait to have you much longer."

Damn it, I hate that we're under the weeping willow tree and it's only mid-afternoon. His erection is pressing against my warm body and I feel the urge to slide my panties over and plunge him into me.

"I know, I was just thinking the same thing. It's just too risky to do it here when everyone is out in the pool in the backyard."

"Fuck that Chloe. I know that is why you wore a dress today….right?"

He gives me a devilish grin and slides me down on his lap toward his knees so that he can release himself from his pants. I watch him intently as he unbuttons the top button to his khaki cargo shorts and I grab his hands. I'm so turned on right now that I can't wait for him to play his little game. I push his hands to the side and slide down his zipper and reach my hands into his shorts.

God damn, Derrick never disappoints me. He's not wearing any underwear which makes this all that much easier. Once he's out all I can do is stare at his beautiful dick. Not that I have a lot to compare it to, but for me it's perfect.

He's perfect.

Derrick watches me and I can tell that he's just as ready as I am to be united as one. He lifts me so that my body is hovering over him. I reach under the hem of my dress and adjust it so that it's just lying below my hips. I pull my panties to the side and quickly force him into me.

The feel of Derrick inside me is like nothing I ever want to let go of…ever. He knows what drives me wild and I know exactly what will push him over the edge. Sometimes we like to take it hard and fast, but times like this we want it soft and slow.

I ride him as he guides my hips up and down, pushing himself in and out of my warmth. He runs his hands along the sides of my body leading to my tits. He massages them with such love until he reaches my taut nipples. He pinches them and I fly over the edge. I can't hold onto this feeling any longer and I let my orgasm take over.

I grab his face in my hands and slide my tongue into his mouth. Our bodies are in sync with one another and I can feel his body shiver as he meets his climax as well. I pull my mouth off of his and look him in the eyes. His baby blues stare into my dark browns and a smile spreads across both of our faces.

"That was wonderful." I whisper.

"That was fucking amazing." He replies.

"How about we go cool off in the pool?"

"I think that's a great idea Chloe."

We pull ourselves together and clean up the picnic mess we've created. Derrick grabs the blanket and picnic basket while I hold the branches to the side so he can exit our tree without getting a face full of weeping willow.

Before going out to the pool we both go into the house and change into our swimming suits. While I wait for Derrick I run into the laundry room and grab us some towels.

I meet him out in the kitchen and we walk hand and hand through the sliding glass door and out onto the deck.

Heading out to the back yard, I can see that Mom, Dad and Char are already out in the pool. Derrick and I make our way over to the pool gate and let ourselves in to join my family.

"Well it's about time you two got out here." Dad says.

"Yeah, what took you so long? It doesn't take four hours to eat lunch." Char says with a giggle.

"Shut the hell up Charlie, I won't see my girl after tomorrow for who knows how long. I needed to soak in as much Chloe time as I can while I have her here with me." Derrick replies.

He throws off his shirt and runs into pool aiming his giant splash right toward my little sister.

"Jerk!" Char screams.

Watching my guy interact with my family like this brings a huge grin to my face. I love everything about him, our relationship and the connection we share. We're going to be just fine, I know it.

DERRICK

I'm sitting in our spot with my girl in my lap. It really is a perfect day that I don't want to end. I wish I could see a few years into the future and know that nothing will change between us. Going off to college and living hundreds of miles apart is going to totally suck, but at this point there isn't much I can do about it. Instead I'm going to enjoy this moment and soak in as much of her as I can while I'm with her.

I can feel her body relaxing against mine and hear her breathing slow. I look down at her and see that she's falling asleep. She looks so comfortable and she's the most beautiful girl I've ever seen. Her dark brown hair is lying across the side of her face and the ends are just long enough that her perky tits are covered. Rather than wake her I decide to soothe her into a deeper sleep by running my fingers up and down her arms.

Shit, she begins to stir and I've had the opposite affect I was hoping for since now she's fully awake. I don't really care what frame she's in as long as she's with me.

Might as well dig right in and play this up while I have the time alone with her. I look over her body as she lies down across my lap. Chloe is fucking gorgeous. Her light complexion is perfect with not a flaw to be found. Her long dark hair frames her perfect face down to her mid back and my god those deep, dark brown eyes are enough to take my breath away.

I lean her forward so that I can move her hair all to one side. A waft of mango hits my nose and I know it's the sweet smelling shampoo and body wash that she uses. It smells so good I have to go in for a lick. I nip at her ear and I pepper kisses along her jaw leading down to her collar bone. She tastes so good. I need to be closer to her and like now.

I never have to ask my girl twice for any type of physical contact. When one of us needs the other, our bodies just tend to go with the flow of the other. I lift her to straddle my legs and I can tell she wants me as much as I want her.

She says it's too risky under our tree, but we've done much worse with fewer clothes in riskier places than her parents' yard.

In no time she's pulling me out of my shorts and the feel of her soft hands on my cock sends a wave of heat through my entire body. She doesn't waste any time and slides her panties to the side allowing her entrance to be ready and waiting for me.

She's so wet. She's always so wet for me. She doesn't just ease me into her she slams herself down on my throbbing dick and I have to slow her down before it's over for both of us. What I wouldn't do to pull this stupid fucking dress right off of her and suck on her sweet little tits.

"Fuck!" I groan.

I slide my hands up her sides and grab onto her breasts. I tweak at her nipples knowing it will build her up to complete her orgasm. I hate to rush this, but there's no way in hell I'm going to last much longer.

Within seconds we're both coming down from our intense climax and I can feel her tight pussy begin to loosen up.

Damn right. Quickies are fucktasitic.

Once we've settled from our 'high' we decide to make our way in the house to get changed and then out to the pool with the rest of her family. Her parents and sister have been so welcoming of me into Chloe's life since we started dating. I feel like I really fit into the Taylor family and know that one day when she truly becomes mine I'll have their full blessing.

As soon as we enter the pool gate, Charlie starts talking up some smack about what was taking us so long under our tree. I know her parents aren't stupid and I'm sure they can figure out what we could have been doing under there, but before the conversations gets any more awkward I decide to jump in and tackle Charlie.

The rest of the day flies by as I spend Chloe's last few hours in Boston with her family. We cook out on the grill for dinner and after Bryce and Teresa suggest we stay in and watch a movie as a family. Chloe and I curl up on the one couch in the family room and I watch as everyone else piles in and takes a seat. As usual Charlie picks the movie and plops herself down on the floor with a huge pillow.

I try to pay attention to the movie, but my mind keeps playing over the fact that Chloe and I are about to move away from one another. I know we'll work through the distance, I just don't want to right now. I love having her close to me, lying against my chest. This is where she needs to be not in fucking New York.

I position my face close to her ear and whisper, "I love you."

I see her cheeks lift into a smile and I feel a warm sensation coating my heart.

She turns her face to look directly into my eyes and says, "I love you too."

This movie must really suck because I honestly have no clue what the hell it's about. That along with the comfort of Chloe's warm body lying against me has me so content that I feel my eyelids getting heavy.

Chloe is already falling asleep, so I grab a blanket from the back of the couch and cover us both up. I lean my head back against the pillow and let my eyes close.

I fall asleep thinking about my future and my life with Chloe.

Chapter 3

CHLOE

My body stirs and I begin to wake. I'm cozy warm and feel a strong arm supporting me along my back. My eyes flutter open and I see Derrick's body lying next to me on the couch. Not quite sure what time it is or when we fell asleep, I look over to the clock hanging on the wall. Oh my god it's 7:30 and today I have to leave…I leave to start the next chapter of my life.

Today is going to be hard walking away from this man, the man that I love with all that I have. It's going to be a test of trust and faith for us to make this work, but I love him so much there's no choice.

I nuzzle my head into his neck and he lets out a sleepy moan. I want to treasure this moment for as long as I can. I inhale his scent and the warmth his body gives off. I move my arms along the side of his body and pull myself in as close as I can. I feel his morning erection up against my belly and smile at the feelings his touch gives me in return.

I know we don't have much time before the family comes down to find us so I have to make these next few moments count.

I slip my hand in between us and gently massage Derrick through his shorts. He moves just enough to allow me room to pull down my shorts and open his button and zipper. A giant smile creeps across my face and in this moment I feel giddy. Even though we're about to be separated by hundreds of miles, this feeling we share when we're together is more than enough to keep me content.

Tilting my head I look into his eyes. He too has a smile plastered to his face as he kisses my forehead. He maneuvers so that he's on top of me and I slide his shorts down just far enough that he's fully exposed to me. Reaching out I grab his perfection and spread my legs on either side of his hips. Ever so gently he pushes himself into me and we begin to rock out a steady motion.

The act of love we are creating is so powerful. My entire body is filled with warmth that only Derrick can provide. I know that I'll never find a man better than this one right here.

Our moment of bliss doesn't last long and I know we need to get ourselves ready for the day we have ahead of us.

"Why don't you go ahead shower and get ready down here and I'll head upstairs. We can meet in the kitchen and cook up some breakfast together." I tell him.

"Sounds great to me." He replies and places a kiss to my lips.

We get up from the couch, a tangled mess of legs and blanket and I make my way down the hall. Reaching the second floor I quickly get into my room, grab up some clothes and enter the bathroom that Char and I share.

When I enter the shower I can hear Char's side of the bathroom door open.

"You ready for today?" She asks.

"As ready as I'll ever be." I reply.

"You know I'm really going to miss you…and Derrick of course."

I can hear the change in Char's voice. We haven't been the best of friends growing up, but we have been the best of sisters.

"You know what Char, I have a job for you while I'm gone that I bet will keep you pretty busy."

"Oh yeah, what's that Chloe?"

"I'm going to be pretty far away from you and Derrick. I need to know that the two of you will be taken care of without me here."

"So what are you saying Chloe…or should I say what are you asking of me? I have my own life too you know and I sure as hell don't have time to babysit your boyfriend." She says with anger in her voice.

"Come on Char. I'm not asking you to babysit him. I just want to know that you're both being looked after. You two are the most important people to me and I need to know that you guys are okay while I'm gone."

She lets out a loud huff and slams her door.

Well that didn't go over as I expected it to, maybe I should have approached Derrick first and let him talk to her about it.

I finish up my shower and hurry getting ready to meet Derrick downstairs.

As I approach the stairs I hear voices in the kitchen. Char seems to be telling Derrick my plan for the two of them while I'm away at school. Well that takes care of that for me. Maybe these two can hash it out better together.

I hop down the stairs and make my way between the two of them to grab a mug of coffee.

"What are you guys talking about?" I ask looking back and forth between the two of them.

"I was just telling Derrick the amazing idea you had for us to keep each other out of trouble while you're gone. He thinks it's just as ridiculous as I do." Char says and sticks her tongue out at me.

"Fine, then just forget I ever mentioned anything. I was just trying to be helpful." I say storming out of the kitchen.

Completely pissed off at Char and Derrick I make my way out to the only place I can hide…our tree.

DERRICK

This morning I wake up to the pleasant feeling of my girlfriend touching my dick through my shorts. She's such a little vixen and I love it, this will have to be fast. Sometimes I just wish I could take us somewhere and hideout for a few days so I can get my Chloe fix…too bad that will never happen.

I kiss the top of her head while she gets in a comfortable position straddling my hips. We find a rhythm that is only meant for us. With a few thrusts and a couple grunts here and there we're done. FUCK! We really need to get a place of our own.

We attempt to untangle ourselves and each head to get a shower before making some breakfast for the family.

Today is D-day for me and I want to show Chloe that I can be supportive and believe that everything will work out for the both of us. We both have bright futures ahead of us and I know that we'll be together through it all.

I make my way up the stairs from the family room into the kitchen where I see Charlie making coffee.

"Morning, Charlie." I say in her direction.

"Hey Derrick, you're here awfully early. Or did you sleep over?" She asks with a cocky smirk.

"Yeah, I did. Guess we fell asleep on the couch and no one felt like waking us up. This worked out just fine with me. I got to cuddle with my Angel all night long." I reply back at her wiggling my eyebrows.

"Hmm, I see." She says giving me an odd look.

"What's your deal? Do I have a bat in the cave? Left or right?" I ask sticking my nose in her face.

"Eww gross Derrick!" She squeals pushing me away.

"Then why are you looking at me like that?" I ask.

"Well your girlfriend thinks we should babysit one another while she's gone, how stupid is that?" She says throwing her head back laughing hysterically.

"Seriously, what the hell does she think we're going to do, run off and join the circus?" I say plopping down on a stool.

"For you, that could be her main concern, you're kind of funny looking." She says with a giggle.

"Shut the hell up Char, you're starting to piss the hell out of me."

Just then Chloe walks into the kitchen grabbing a coffee mug. She's dressed in a simple sundress and she has her long dark hair in waves falling along her back. She looks over and catches me staring at her. With her beautiful brown eyes she gives me a wink asking what Charlie and I are talking about.

Charlie of course opens her big mouth with an attitude and Chloe runs out of the kitchen and into the backyard.

"Nice job Charlie, she's fucking leaving today. Can't you keep the peace for one fucking day?" I say grabbing up two mugs of hot coffee and on my way outside to find Chloe.

Walking toward our tree I can hear Chloe's muffled cry.

I do my best to get to her so that I can calm her down without spilling coffee all over me. Damn this shit is hot.

When I finally reach her she's sitting on the bench with her head in her hands crying.

"Love, don't cry, please don't cry." I say approaching her.

Setting down the hot mugs on a side table, I grab her up into my arms and sit down on the bench.

"Look, Charlie and I are just playing around. We know you care about us and that we'll need each other to get through this time. I promise you that Charlie will be fine. She's a big girl and can take care of herself. As for me, you know I'd never do anything stupid to hurt what we have."

"I know it's just really hard to leave my two favorite people." She says in between sobs.

"Come on, we knew this day was going to come and I'm not going sit here with you and mope."

I pull her hair back away from her face and lay it between her shoulders. With my thumbs I wipe away her tears and place a soft kiss on her nose.

"I love you Chloe. Now pull your shit together so we can enjoy the last few hours of you in Boston." Handing her a mug of coffee.

"God Derrick, one day you're going to be a fine ass lawyer. I love it when you get all bossy." She giggles and takes in a sip of steaming French vanilla coffee.

"Yes I am, now let's go make some food. I'm starving."

I pull Chloe up from the bench and hold her hand while we walk across the lawn and into the house. By the time we get inside Char, Teresa and Bryce are already fixing up breakfast. I take a seat at the breakfast bar and finish up my morning brew.

"Okay Chloe, we only have an hour or so till we hit the road. Are you all ready to go?" Bryce asks.

I look at Bryce and then over to Chloe. My stomach does a flip flop and then plummets down to my toes. I was hoping this feeling wouldn't start until she got in the car and drove off.

"Yeah Daddy, I'm ready. It's just going to suck saying goodbye, ya know?" She says looking me straight in the eyes.

"We all know it's going to be hard sweetie, but you'll be home for the holidays in a few months." Teresa says with a cheery smile.

I sit and watch the conversation that is taking place in front of me and I feel like a lead weight is holding me down on the bar stool. Being here is the only place I want to be, but it's going to tear out my heart to watch her drive off in her parents' SUV.

"Well let's eat up here and get a move on. We have quite the drive today." Bryce tells the girls.

I grab my plate and fill it up with food. In this moment I'm not only weighted down, I'm beginning to feel numb. How is any of this possible? I mean I'm a tough as nails jock and I feel like my world is crashing in around me. A serious reality check is needed. Maybe after they leave I'll head over to the gym or go for a run.

Tomorrow is my day to drive out to Cambridge so I need to get my head on straight before practice and classes start.

The family finishes up breakfast and I help clean up the mess and dishes. Chloe goes up to her room to grab some last minute things and comes down with a big smile on her face.

"Okay kids let's shake a leg and get a move on here." Bryce says while patting me on the back.

"Yeah, um, I'm not going to take the drive with you guys this time. I've still got a ton of stuff to pack myself so I'll be saying my goodbye now." I reply to not just Bryce, but to the whole family.

I walk Chloe to the front door as the rest of the crew head out toward the garage. She grabs my hand and wraps it around her waist. I look into her deep brown eyes and tears begin to roll down her cheeks. Without saying a word she lets her body talk for her. She puts both arms around my neck and pulls me in for a kiss. This isn't like any other kiss, it's much more. With our lips connected and our tongues intertwined we're sharing what we feel, how our touch releases warmth over our bodies and the fear we share of missing one another.

I run my arms up and down her back letting every last touch trigger memories for us that will last till we see each other again.

Pulling away from her embrace I see her brow furrow and I place my finger to her lips.

"Don't do it Chloe, don't say goodbye. I'll see you as soon as we have our schedules figured out. We'll never say goodbye, instead it's see you later."

She nods her head in agreement and gives me one last kiss on the lips.

We walk out the front door and over to her mom's Expedition. I hold her hand and help her up into the back. Once she's in her seat I hand her a card and she does the same. We both laugh at the corny things we do for one another.

Blowing her one last kiss I tell her to call me once she gets there.

"See you later Angel." I say as I wave.

I watch Bryce back the SUV down the driveway and meet Charlie up on the porch.

My Chloe is gone and now all I can do is think about when I'll see her, smell her and touch her next.

Chapter 4
Four years later
May 2009

CHLOE

Walking through each room, I'm swarmed with great memories. Tears begin to swell in my eyes and I'm suddenly filled with an emotion of sadness as I walk past the living room and out onto the balcony. I'm the last of my roommates to clean out of the apartment. The other girls have gotten jobs in the city and will be staying in New York. Lucky for them their moving day was a lot less of a drive than mine will be today.

I can't believe this day is already here. It feels like yesterday mom and dad where driving me to New York for freshman orientation and today I'm graduating from NYU. A lot has happened over the past four years, but one thing is for certain I'll cherish the friendships I've made. Living away from home was a bit of a struggle at first, but luckily I had some great people around me for support. For the past few years we've stuck by each other's sides and made friendships I know will last a lifetime.

Coming back inside I shut the sliding glass doors and turn the lock for the last time. I head over to the oversized suede chair in the middle of the room and take a seat. I close my eyes for brief moment and watch as my memories of college slide past my eyelids. NYU has given me everything I had hoped it would not to mention a strong list of recommendations to head out into the work force. My dream job is to become a sports analyst for ESPN, but I know I'll have to start small and work my way up. I had a great internship opportunity this past year and it gave me the knowledge and skills I'll need to land a job back in Boston. Now all I need to do is find that job and start living my life.

After a few more minutes of reminiscing and planning my future, I decide to get dressed.

I'm so excited for today. As I get ready for graduation in my empty apartment all I can think about is that I can't wait to see Derrick. He should be here any moment to pick me up. Having him in New York with me today just makes everything perfect. It's been a few weeks since I last saw him, so there's no telling if I'll be able to keep my hands to myself when he arrives.

I was so worried that our relationship would be destroyed when going off to college, but the best part of all is that the distance just made us that much stronger as a couple. There really isn't anything that could tear the two of us apart. Between my travels to Cambridge for home football games and Derrick coming down to NYU after the football season was over, we were lucky to see each other at least once a month.

A light off beat tapping noise comes from the hallway and I can only imagine the games this man is willing to play. He just loves to make me crazy. I pretend not to hear anything and continue getting myself ready. Then it hits me that he might be here with his parents. With that thought I bust a move and head for the door. I sure as hell don't want to piss off Rose and Bud.

I'm so glad they are all here for me today. Fortunately for both our families Derrick and my graduation ceremonies were scheduled a week apart. This gives us the opportunity to have everyone in New York this weekend and then everyone back in Massachusetts for Derrick's graduation next week.

"Well hello there Angel, you look breathtaking as usual." Derrick says coming through the doorway and kissing me on the cheek.

He looks absolutely delicious in his black suit. I want to jump in his arms and swing my legs up around his hips, but with his parents following behind I don't think that would be too appropriate.

"Yes she does look absolutely beautiful, congratulations Chloe. We're so proud of you." Rose says pulling me in for a hug.

"Thank you so much for being here today. It's amazing to have both of our families in New York this weekend."

"Are you ready Chloe, because we don't want you being late to your graduation breakfast? We told Bryce and Teresa we'd get you there on time." Bud says.

"Dad chill, we have plenty of time to make it to the restaurant." Derrick says trying to calm his dad down.

Derrick's parents are great. They've always been very welcoming of me and our relationship.

"Don't worry Bud, I promise I won't make us late. I just need to finish a few things and then we can go."

"Chloe love, do you need any help in there?" Derrick asks.

"Please Derrick let the poor girl get herself ready." Rose says holding onto Derrick's shoulder.

"Mom, I haven't seen my girl in weeks. I need to take advantage of all the time I have with her."

"It's okay Rose. I missed him too. He can come help me apply my makeup if he wants." I say with a giggle.

"Yes! Thanks Angel, let's do this." Derrick says clasping his hands together.

Derrick is such a dork, he'll do just about anything to get some alone time with me.

After much trial and error with the supporting hands and lips of Derrick, I'm able to apply and reapply my lipstick only five times before leaving my bathroom. Finally we're able to make our way back to his parents and not be late meeting my family for breakfast.

DERRICK

Breakfast with the Taylor and Peters families is a good time as always. It's great having all of us in one room. I can only imagine how things will be when we gather like this with a family of our own. Chloe and I've been talking about marriage since before we left for college so it really isn't a question of if I'll propose, it's more like when.

After breakfast we make our way over to the college. Our families head into the stadium to take their seats and I go with Chloe to find a few of her friends who she'll be sitting with for the ceremony.

I've met her roommates and friends during the times I came down to visit her in New York so I feel like part of their inner circle. Everyone seems to be excited about graduation and moving on with their careers, but I can tell Chloe is not one hundred percent into the conversation.

I rub my hand up and down the back of her graduation gown and give her a kiss on the cheek.

She turns to look at me with those big brown eyes and I see a hint of sadness.

"You okay love?" I ask pulling her into an embrace.

"Yeah, I'm good. I just wish I had things lined up like the girls do. Everyone else seems to have landed a permanent job with their internships or found something else. I've got nothing to move onto now that school is out and you're going to law school in the fall. What do I have to look forward to Derrick?"

I look back into her eyes and a few tears spill out of those gorgeous browns.

"Don't you worry about that stuff now Chloe. Today is your day and I sure as hell don't want you upset when you walk across that stage. Your life will go on once you're back in Boston. That's the choice you made and I know you'll find something. If you chose to stay in New York you'd be in a job already. Don't doubt yourself Angel, you're going to make things happen, I just know it."

With that I kiss her on the lips and hear the ushers telling the class to go line up.

"Well it's show time. I'll see you in a few hours. Don't trip when you cross the stage. I'd hate to have to run down there and make a scene to cover for you."

Chloe giggles and wraps her arms around my neck.

"You're amazing Derrick and I love you."

"Love you too."

The entire commencement ceremony passes by in a blur. There are a few hundred students walking today and I totally spaced out during the speakers. I'm too anxious to get back to Chloe's empty apartment. She just needs to grab her last minute things and then we can head home to Boston. It's all I've thought about over the past few weeks. Really, it's all I've looked forward to, to get me through missing her when we weren't together.

Her parents arranged for the moving truck to deliver Chloe's things to her parents' house Monday. This way we don't have to rush back to Boston after the commencement. There were only a few larger pieces of furniture that they would need to pick up, but for the most part Chloe had all her valuable things in a few boxes we were able to fit into our cars.

Bryce and Teresa drove with Charlie back in their Expedition and my parents were planning to follow in the Range Rover. With two pretty big SUV's there wasn't too much little stuff for the movers to pick up.

Chloe decided she'd drive back home with me and my parents so that we could be together. I wasn't going to argue with her since I too wanted the time to spend with her. By the time we hit the highway Chloe was nestled into my side and falling fast asleep.

I ran my fingers up and down her back to help her feel comfortable and within a few minutes she was fast asleep with a slight grin on her face.

If only she knew how glad I was that we had made it this far. The last four years were great, but still it was a struggle not to see her as much as I would've liked. Chloe is my world and I want to make her happy and feel safe with who we are and where our relationship is going.

I was a content man heading back home with his girl. A girl that one day would be my wife.

I rented a small townhouse in between Boston and Cambridge so that I'm close to school and Chloe. Since she hasn't found a job yet, she felt it would be best to stay with her parents and make it a focus to sell herself to the local new stations. I know once she gets herself in the right frame of mind she'll make it somewhere, it's just going to be hard for a little while. The good thing is that we'll be home in Boston together and I can support her as much as she needs.

It feels good to say go home to Boston, in fact I love knowing that I'll be there with Chloe. Finally after four years we'll be together without having to miss one another for more than a day. It's almost as if I'm in a fucking dream. I never thought this day would come…now I never have to be apart from her again and we can start the future we've always talked about.

Chapter 5
August 2009

CHLOE

    The past few weeks have been absolutely amazing. Having the summer to enjoy my family and friends was exactly what I needed after being away for four years. Now that graduation is past me and I've had a few months of fun in the sun, it's time to find a job. When I came back from school I scouted a few places I'd like to work so my goal this week is to get my portfolio and resume together. But before I crack down on the job hunt I have one more day of relaxation. So I'm off to Derrick's for one last fun day.

We decided to spend today on Derrick's boat with our families. It's the last day of summer for Derrick since he's starting law school tomorrow. This will be a great way to bring an end to our summertime bliss and prepare for the next few months ahead.

I chose to drive over to Derrick's place on my own and meet my family over at the marina. This makes the most sense to me since I'll be staying over at Derrick's tonight, like I pretty much do every other night anyway.

Derrick has been up my ass asking me to move into his condo, but I'd rather wait till I know I can contribute somehow. I know he wants to take care of me and can handle the expenses, but still I'd feel better knowing we're in it together.

When I arrive at Derrick's condo he's sitting at his desk in the living room with his Red Sox ball cap on backwards. He turns to face me and looks at me like he wants to attack.

He looks way too good to just be going sailing. I think I'd rather stay home all day and admire the man sitting in front of me.

"You have that look in your eye again Derrick. I don't want to have to explain anymore bruises on my ass." I tell him plopping down on his super comfy couch.

"Oh come on Angel that wasn't my fault you fell off the bed and hurt your little ass. Maybe next time you'll be more careful and won't have to walk around funny cause your ass hurts."

"Well if you wouldn't have been tickling me like you were I wouldn't have fallen off of your bed."

"I beg to differ with you love. All I wanted was for you to say yes to move in with me. Since you continue to say no, I think it's best that I torture you somehow."

I start to giggle as I watch him cross the room to come stand in front of me by the couch.

"What's so funny Chloe?" He asks running his fingers through my waves and taking a seat next to me.

"Nothing is funny except for you and your persistence. I love you, you know that?"

"I do, so move in with me."

"Oh god Derrick, I told you I would as soon as I find a job."

Derrick pouts like a little kid that just lost his best friend. It's time for a subject change, if nothing else he'll be pouncing on me in no time.

"So are you ready for your first day of law school tomorrow?" I ask.

"Yep, I can't believe I'm going back to school for another three years." He says with a laugh.

"Well just think after those three years you'll be a lawyer."

"Yeah, right after I pass the bar exam in three years." He says looking down at the ground.

"You will, I have faith in you and your smarts." I say with a wink.

Derrick really is one of the smartest people I know and has accomplished so much in his life already. Becoming a lawyer has always been a dream of his since he was young. His Papa was a well known lawyer in the Boston area and after he passed away Derrick made it his mission to follow in Papa's footsteps. I really do admire him for his goals and the way he goes about achieving everything he sets out to do. Sometimes he puts way too much pressure on himself, but now I'm here to support him through the next three years and I feel really good about that.

"You ready to hit the road and meet up with everyone at the marina." I ask.

"Sure, let's just load up the car and we'll get going." He replies still pouting.

"Hey don't be a piss head today, Derrick. Everything will work out don't stress about it okay. Today is supposed to be fun. Smile…for me?"

I turn to face him and wrap my arms around his neck. He still has a pout on his face and his beautiful baby blues look so sad. I touch my lips to his and give him a kiss that will hopefully snap him out of his mood. He returns the kiss sliding his tongue into my mouth and grabbing my ass. I giggle in his embrace and feel a grin spread across his handsome face.

"Now that's much better." I say pulling away to look at his smile.

"Well if you would kiss me like that all day and let me have my way, I'd never stop smiling." He replies with a devilish smirk.

"You keep pushing pal and just wait and see what happens."

"Oh Chloe, is that a promise?" He asks.

"You'll just have to find out later tonight." I say running my finger down his chest and grab the waistband of his shorts.

"Shit Chloe, you make me crazy. How am I supposed to drive and go meet our parents when you keep making my dick hard like this?"

"Think baseball love and let's go." I tell him while walking out the garage door to his car.

"You suck Chloe!" He shouts after me.

"Yes I do and if I recall you enjoy it when I do." I giggle tossing the bags into his car.

Love.

It's a simple four letter word that is easy to pass through the lips but hard to say it to a person…unless that person is Chloe Taylor. I love her more than any man has ever loved another woman and I feel so lost without her. She's been my best friend for nearly my entire life. We've gone through some pretty crazy times as friends, but nothing has meant more to me than the past four years as her boyfriend. I love spending time with her whether it's with our families, our friends or just hanging alone with her. She consumes me with her eyes, her fiery touch and the ways in which she loves me.

This summer has been fucktastic. Chloe and I have spent just about every day together and I couldn't have asked for anything better, that's unless she'd agree to move in with me. I'm not going to lie, I like playing house with her. I enjoy waking up with her body curled into mine. It's better than I could ever have imagined, but she refuses to move in with me permanently until she finds a job. Believe me I get where she's coming from, but I don't see why she can't move in and look for a job at the same time.

She makes me want to be a better man but at the same time bang my head against the wall till my eyes roll out. I just can't get enough of her and when she has to go home I toss and turn all night without her…it just sucks. It really fucking blows.

I need to pry myself out of this funk before she gets here. If she sees me in a mood she's going to exhaust herself trying to make me feel better. If she'd just listen to me and let me get my own way once in a while all this shit would be past us.

Today we're taking the Taylor and Peters crew out on the sail boat for a day of peace and relaxation before I start back to school tomorrow. This is just what we need to close out the summer in style. A nice day, some good food and a few adult beverages…perfect.

The door opens and I can hear her footsteps and smell coffee.

I turn to see her standing there in a fitted Red Sox tee and tiny white shorts. Just looking at her has my heart pounding in my chest and my shorts feeling tighter around my dick. Damn this girl does things to me.

She comments about the look I'm giving her and I can only tease her back. I love the way my intensity effects her. We banter back in forth about the fact that she refuses to move in with me and it puts me back in a pissed off mood. If this girl would just let me get my own way and allow me to take care of her everything would just be perfect. But of course Chloe is a strong and independent woman, it's one of the reasons I love her so much.

I manage to load the food and bags into the car with the massive hard on Chloe gave me. Too bad I have to wait till later tonight for her to help me release the pent up pressure of my now aching blue balls.

We pull into the marina just in time to meet up with our families. Everyone greets one another with hugs and then helps bring all the goods down to the boat. With assistance from Bryce and my dad we're set to sail the lake in no time and the ladies prepare the spread of food to keep us going for the day. Once the sails are hoisted it's time to kick back and relax.

I can hear the banter going on among the group and I have to laugh at the topics of conversation. Dad and Bryce are chatting up about the Red Sox making the playoffs and mom, Teresa, Charlie and Chloe are discussing the appropriate clothing Chloe should wear when she's on TV. I shake my head at all of them and try to choose where I want to join in. Since the guys seem to be having an important conversation, I decide to break up the women's chatter.

"So ladies are we having fun yet?" I ask sitting down next to Chloe.

I put my arm around her shoulders and pull her into my embrace. Kissing the top of her head I can smell her sweet mango shampoo and suddenly I'm fully relaxed.

"Yes honey of course we're having a good time. Are you?" Mom asks me.

"Yup." I reply stretching out my legs and leaning back against the side of the boat.

"This really is a beautiful day to be out on the lake. Thanks again for inviting us Derrick." Teresa says.

"Chloe and I figured we might as well spend the last day of summer out here with all of you. Once classes start up and Chloe goes to work, I don't know how much free time we'll have to spend together as a family."

Chloe turns and smiles at me as I rub my hand up and down her back. Looking at her my mind is at peace and I know that I'm the luckiest man in the world to be by her side. Everything has worked out for us. Through all of our struggles, between the stress of school and the distance we were apart, our relationship only grew to be stronger. The next few years will be just as good because Chloe will be there to help me get through the rough patches and I'll be there to do the same for her.

The next stage of our lives is already paved out for us. Now all we have to do is put our best foot forward and make it happen. There's no doubt in my mind that this woman and I are meant to be together and the day I graduate from law school is the day I'll ask her to be mine forever.

Chapter 6
January 2010

CHLOE

Finally giving into Derricks need for me to live with him, I made the decision to move into his condo after the holidays. Since I've been working for the local news agency, WZDH Channel 7, I figure it's time to make our living arrangement more permanent. Besides, I'm practically living here anyway.

"Moving is absolute hell, well at least for me it is." I complain to Char.

"Chloe, it really isn't going to be that bad. More than half of your shit is already at Derrick's condo." She replies.

"Yeah, I know that. It still sucks having to pack up everything here at mom and dad's house and then move it over there."

"Then why not hire a mover?" She asks.

"Nah, I don't have enough shit for that."

"Ugh, you drive me crazy Chloe. What can I help you with while I'm here?"

Thankfully Char is the nicer sister out of the two of us and she helps me pack up my room in less than two hours. Now I just need Derrick to come over with his parent's SUV so we can load it all up and get a move on. Moving is not one of my favorite things to do and although I don't have a lot of stuff, I still feel like it's taking forever.

"Look, see that wasn't so bad now was it?" Char asks.

"For you maybe not, I just hate doing this stuff."

"Well at least we're done."

I look up and see Derrick walking into my bedroom. He's wearing an old Palmer High School tee-shirt and a pair of sweat pants that are riding low on his hips. Taking a mental picture of this man is a must. How can he look so good on the day we're moving. He comes over to me and grabs my hands to pull me up off the floor.

"You look hot today." He says.

Char lets out a loud laugh and walks out of the room shaking her head.

"Come on Derrick, I'm a mess and haven't even showered today."

"I don't care. You still look cute in your sweats and your hair falling out of this pony tail.

Derrick grabs at my pony tail holder and pulls it from my hair.

I shake my hair loose and it falls into my face.

"That better?" I ask.

"Holy shit! We better get this stuff back to our place so I can have my way with you."

"Yeah sounds good. But only if we can start in the shower." I say with a giggle and a wink in his direction.

Derrick pulls me in close to his body and nips at my lower lip and then slides his tongue into my mouth.

"Yum, you taste good love. Let's get this stuff in the SUVs before I can't move from this hard on."

I punch him in the arm and grab a box to carry downstairs.

"Well let's go Derrick. The faster we move now, the slower we can take it later."

"Damn it Chloe, you're killing me." He replies while grabbing three boxes, stacking them and running past me down the stairs and out the front door.

"Whoa there killer, what has him in such a hurry all of a sudden?" Char asks.

I laugh at her question and follow Derrick out the door with Char on my heels. "Let's just say I gave him an incentive to hurry up and get us home."

"I don't even want to know…do I?" Char asks.

"Probably not little sis." I reply with a giggle.

In a half hour, Derrick, Char and I have the Range Rover and Expedition packed and ready to head over to the condo. Char decides to tag along in her own car to help us unload. What a great kid sister I have. Really, she's always there to lend a hand and I can always count on her when I'm in need of a friend. We've grown a bit closer now that I'm home from school. I just hope me moving out of the house doesn't push us back apart.

We all arrive at the condo one vehicle following the other into the driveway. Feeling tired from all this moving I just really want to get these boxes in the house and relax for the rest of the day. But knowing Derrick, he'll want to organize where this shit should go right away. Maybe I can coerce him to wait till tomorrow if I offer him sex. I can always persuade him with some hanky panky. Yes that's exactly what I'll do.

Derrick doesn't hesitate to wait for Char or me to approach. He just starts to grab boxes and move them into the house. Damn it, there goes that idea of waiting to put them where they belong. Oh well, guess I better help out and get this shit put away. Then I'm showering and relaxing with him for the rest of the weekend. I think

I like that plan much better. Derrick always knows what is best for me, even when we don't communicate verbally. I'm one lucky lady.

Watching Derrick run in and out of the house with boxes makes me laugh. He's still motivated by our early conversation and I can only love him that much more that he's busting his ass knowing sex is waiting for him.

"Seriously Chloe, did he chug an energy drink on the way over here? I don't think I've ever seen him move that fast. Not even on the football field." Char says.

The expression on her face and her comment makes me laugh so hard I double over. Derrick comes running out of the house and over to us. His face is flushed and sweat is dripping down his face. Even though it's freezing outside I can still see that he's sweating under his sweatshirt.

"What the hell is so funny ladies?" He asks wiping his brow and taking a swig of his water bottle.

"Char asked what has you in such a hurry to unpack the boxes and I just had to laugh."

Derrick throws his arm around my waist and picks me up like I'm a football.

"Well Char, you see. Your sister told me the faster I got her moved in the slower I can fuck her later."

"Oh my god, I think I just threw up in my mouth." Char says holding her hands in front of her face.

"Shut the hell up Char. I'm plenty sure Marc has his way with you when you two are alone." Derrick says while carrying me into the house.

"Regardless of what I do with my boyfriend, you surely don't need to tell me about you and my sister's sex life." Char says.

Derrick continues to carry me through the house and sits me down on the kitchen countertop. Even with their banter, I know that Derrick and Char love each other like brother and sister, they sure as hell fight like they're related.

"Can I get you something to eat or drink before you head home Char?" Derrick asks handing me a bottle of water and an apple.

"Nah, I'm good. Do you guys need anything else before I head out?"

I hop down off the counter and walk over to her giving her a big hug. "Thanks for all your help Char. It means a lot that you helped us out today."

"No worries Chloe. Well I better get going. I'm heading back to school tonight to go to Marc's frat party. See you guys next weekend."

"Love you Char." Derrick and I say in unison.

"Love you guys too." She says with a wave and is out the door.

DERRICK

The past few months have mentally exhausted me and to think I have two and half more years of law school. Becoming a lawyer is something I've wanted since I was younger. I knew it was my calling and I wanted to make my Papa proud. My parents told me I could be whatever I wanted while I was growing up, but I felt like I was destined to do this.

I knew that my courses would be challenging and believe me I love to bust my ass, but the next few years are going to give me a run for my money.

Today, however, is the day I've been anticipating for five and half years. Ever since Chloe and I started dating I wanted to take her away and keep her for myself forever. Now we're making things a little more permanent by her finally agreeing to move into my condo. It makes a lot of sense for us. She pretty much stays here every night anyway. But now she's going to be here for good. I love the idea of knowing I can wake up every morning and she'll be right there for me to curl into her warm body. Even better she'll be here every night for me to fall asleep with.

I make my way over to her parent's house to grab the last few things she should be packing. We worked it out that her mom would take Chloe's car today in exchange for the Expedition and I did the same with my mom. Having the two larger vehicles will hopefully mean we can get this all done in one trip. Tomorrow we'll worry about switching cars back to their rightful owners.

Walking up the stairs to Chloe's room I hear her and Char chatting. I look into her bedroom and see that they are both sitting on the floor amongst a floor filled with boxes. Chloe sits there looking exhausted, but there's still something that makes her look irresistible. She's wearing black yoga pants and pink GAP hoodie. Her dark brown hair is somewhat pulled up into a ponytail, but for the most part it's falling out in pieces around her face. She actually looks hot.

I catch her giving me a once over and no doubt she's thinking some dirty thoughts herself. We're such a pair.

Now to get her stuff packed into the cars and over to our place.

Within record time Charlie, Chloe and I have loaded and unloaded both SUVs and now my girl is fully moved into our condo. I'm beyond excited to live with Chloe and start our lives together.

After Charlie leaves Chloe and I decide to make some sandwiches to eat.

"So this is your first official meal in your new house, pretty good right?"

"Derrick if this is how you're going to feed me now that we're living together I might as well not unpack." She says with a smile.

"Shit, I guess I should have planned better and made you a full five course meal for your first night in your new home." I say smiling right back at her.

"Yeah, guess you should have." She says with a pout.

"Oh man Chloe, I know you're playing with me now, but I'm sure there's some way I can make it up to you." I say.

I watch her respond to me as she looks up through her thick lashes and gives me a killer smile. We both know what is going to happen next. But at the same time we enjoy torturing the hell out of one another making the other wait to see who will break first.

"Hmm, well Derrick you did upset me." She says continuing to give me an adorable pout.

"Bullshit sweetheart. But I'll play along anyway. I can call your bluff."

"I hope whatever you have in mind is really good." She continues to say while standing up from the kitchen stool right in front of me.

Chloe puts her hands on my forearms and slides them up to my neck. She pulls me in closer to her, but keeps her face far enough away that I can't reach her lips with mine. I want to taste her, to kiss her, but at the same time I want to see where she goes with this when I give her the control.

"Oh love, I've hurt your feelings. You know I love you more than anything. What can I do to make it all up to you?" I ask pushing my hips into hers.

I continue to lean against her body until she's stopped by the kitchen countertop. The way this woman has me, there's no way she can't feel the arousal springing through my sweatpants and against her body. I brace us against the cabinets and put an arm on either side of her body. She looks at me with desire in her eyes and that gives me the push to make the next move. I smash my mouth against hers sliding my tongue into her mouth. Chloe lets out a moan and I pull her forward grabbing her ass and lifting her so that her legs are wrapped around my hips. We kiss for what feels like forever and then we pull apart taking in deep breaths.

"Hmm well I think you can start by helping me get cleaned up from this day of moving."

"Hell yeah Angel, off to the shower we go." I reply.

Chloe giggles in my ear and pulls her arms in closer around my neck. I pick up my walking pace and hurry back to our bedroom and connecting bathroom. I'm going to make this shower a quick one because I plan on enjoying her for the rest of the day in our bed.

Chapter 7
Two years later
January 2012

CHLOE

The past two years have been a little chaotic to say the least. Between Derrick busting his ass with classes, working more than part time at a local law firm and me traveling around to cover the Red Sox's season we barely have time to breathe. So what else do we do? The two crazy nuts we are decide to buy a house. It seems like a logical investment for us both. We love living in the Boston area and feel it's only smart to buy as opposed to throwing away our money on the condo every month.

We've looked around for a few months but nothing really caught our attention until we saw this one. This house caught both of our eyes. It's in a new development a few miles outside the city of Boston so our commutes are not too long. The structure of the house is two stories with a full finished basement. The basement has three rooms and bathroom, which is perfect for me to have an office downstairs and Derrick to have his man cave. On the first floor there's a living room, dining room, kitchen and half bath. The second floor has three bedrooms rather than just two which works for when we need the extra space. The house sits on a quarter acre lot that backs up to a wooded area. Everything about this house screams home to both Derrick and I.

I take a seat at the breakfast nook and let out a deep sigh, finally we're settled and the last of the boxes have been taken out to the garage. Taking a sip of my wine I glance at my watch. Hmm, it's 9:30. I better get started on a few things before Derrick gets home. For the past week I have done my best to get this house organized while Derrick is working some late nights at the firm. I give him all the credit in the world. I really don't know how he has the energy to do everything he does and then come home and work some more. After school is all said and done I know it will all have been worth it to him, but in the meantime I feel like he's going to burn out.

He should be home any minute so I place his already prepared dinner in the microwave and pull out a bottle of beer. After setting the table for him I set a place for myself just so he doesn't have to eat alone. Our time together has been pretty limited over the past few months, but we still make up for it with the time we do have to spend together.

I hear the garage door open and suddenly feel a bit giddy. Derrick still has a way of making me act like a love sick school girl when he's near me. I don't think I'll ever lose that feeling. He really is the best guy and I'm lucky as hell that he's stuck by me for the past few years.

Derrick comes in the house and tosses his briefcase on the living room chair. I watch as he walks around the room inching toward the kitchen. He looks absolutely gorgeous wearing a button down blue dress shirt that fits his toned body perfectly and a nice pair of khaki pants. As he approaches the kitchen he runs his hand through his perfectly styled hair and catches me staring at him. The color of the shirt makes his baby blue eyes stand out like crazy. He comes closer to me with a big smile on his face.

"There's my Angel. How was your day Chloe?" He asks pulling me into his embrace.

He smells like clean laundry, a mixture of his scented cologne and body wash. Mmm I love the way he smells.

"Hey love, my day was boring. But now you're here so it's much better." I say with a smile and a kiss to his lips.

"Yeah, I agree the day just got a hundred times better when I pulled into the driveway and saw you were home."

Derrick returns my kiss and walks us back up against the fridge while running his hands up and down my back finally grabbing onto my ass.

"Yes much better indeed." He says with a smirk.

I kiss him again on the lips and then move over to the microwave that is now beeping.

"I heated dinner for you. Why don't you take a seat in the dining room and I'll bring everything in for you? Do you have a lot of work to do tonight?"

"Thanks Chloe. No actually I didn't have any work to bring home tonight. I was hoping to just spend the night with you."

I bring out his plate of food and the bottle of beer setting it down in front of him. He grabs onto my hips and positions me into his lap. He moves my hair to the side so that he has better access to my neck and begins to pepper kisses at my collar bone, along my jaw and turning my face he kisses my lips.

"How about I skip dinner and we head to the bedroom for some dessert?" I giggle in his neck and twitch in his lap. I can feel he's more than ready to move onto the dessert course of the evening, but this poor guy has to eat dinner too.

"As much as I want to get to bed with you, I still want you to eat your dinner. Then we can get to dessert. Deal?" I ask kissing the tip of his nose.

"Yes!" He shouts and shoves me off his lap.

I laugh at the crazy that is Derrick as he shovels forkfuls of noodles into his mouth. I really do love this man. I continue to watch him plow through his dinner and sit next to him sipping my wine.

DERRICK

Today has been a long and stressful day. Not like the last two years haven't, but today especially has been one of those days.

I can't help but feel a little nervous to get home tonight. Never in the time we've been together have I kept something from Chloe, but this…this I have to try my best to keep a secret, at least for another few months. Once law school is over I'll do it. I'll be able to tell her everything.

The knot in my stomach is growing the closer I get to the house. Ugh, our house. Yes the house we just bought together. This is the place I envision spending the rest of my life with Chloe and where we will start building a family. I met with someone today and the choice I made will change things forever. It will change where Chloe and I stand and where we've been for the past few years

I'm only a few minutes from home and I know I need to pull my shit together. The past two years have been hard on both of us and I don't need to bring in more drama to the table. In less than six months I'll be graduating from Harvard Law, pass the Massachusetts bar and be brought on full time at the Jax & Paige law firm. Yeah this is all going to work out, no doubt.

I pull into the driveway and Chloe's car is already in the garage. I haven't spoken to her since this morning, but I assumed she would still be at the studio finishing the segment from tonight's game.

Walking into the house I toss my briefcase onto the leather chair in the living room and make my way toward the kitchen. My head is pounding and I attempt to relieve some tension by running my hands through my hair. I can smell spaghetti in the air and hear the microwave running. So sweet, Chloe saved me dinner. Not like it really surprises me she's been doing this a lot for me lately.

My gaze shifts from the floor up to the sexiest pair of legs, then up to her tits and finally landing on those beautiful brown eyes. A smile splits my face and all other worries from a few moments ago are gone. Chloe helps to calm me. She makes me feel like nothing in this world exists other than the two of us. I love her more than anything and one day she'll be all mine.

I pull Chloe into my arms and a sense of warmth and love take over my body. Being with her simply relaxes me and thank god tonight I don't have work to do before bed. Tonight is just going to be me and my girl.

Chloe brings me my dinner and a beer out to the dining room and I pull her into my lap. I smell her sweet scent of mango and begin to kiss her. I love having her close to me and I can't get enough of my lips on her skin.

As I play around with her, only really arousing myself, she makes a deal with me that if I eat my dinner like a good boy I can have her for dessert later. I'm all up for the challenge. I push her off of my lap and go to town eating the spaghetti on my plate. Chloe laughs at me, and shakes her head. But deep down I know she loves it.

Once I have finally finished dinner I clean up my dishes and pull Chloe up from her chair in the dining room.

"I'm ready for my desserts now love." I say taking a nip of her bottom lip.

"Dear god Derrick, after you ate all that how could you possibly have room for dessert?"

"Oh I have plenty of room for the kind of desserts I have in mind."

She giggles and allows me to lead her through our house and into our bedroom. I'm shocked when I enter our room.

"Shit Chloe! When did you do all this?" I look around our bedroom and see a completely different site than what I had left this morning.

Chloe has decorated our bedroom into a tranquil room for us to relax in after a tiring day at work. The black, white and blue colors are so vibrant and they blend so well with the dark furniture we chose to buy the other day.

I look her in the eyes and she has a smile on her face. She looks pleased with herself.

"Yep." She replies.

"When did you have the time to finish unpacking the room? It looks great." I ask.

When I left this morning, our room was still full of boxes and we were sleeping on the mattresses piled on the floor. Now it looks as though someone came in and completely redesigned our room after going through our moving boxes.

She hops onto our king size sleigh bed and pats the mattress down beside her for me to come and sit. I follow her gesture and hop myself right down next to her.

"I had mom and dad come over after work today to help me. I wanted to surprise you. Our room was the last room to be unpacked and since you've been coming home exhausted every day, I wanted to do this for you."

I grab her face in my hands and kiss her hard on the lips. I don't need the world. I surely don't need materialistic things. But the things that this girl does for me make me so happy.

"Thank you Chloe. It looks amazing in here. I don't want to go all girly on you but really I love what you have done with this room. It feels so peaceful and calming. The colors are perfect to help me relax after a rough day at school and work. I love you Angel, thank you."

"You're welcome Derrick. Now why don't I help you get out of that shirt and pants? Then you can really show me how much you appreciate my work today."

"I'm all yours love, do your worst." I say standing with my hands raised in the air.

She can have me anyway she wants me, her wish is my command.

"Oh I will. Come here lover boy." She says pulling at the waist of my pants pulling me down onto the bed.

Chapter 8
May 2012

CHLOE

Today is one of the most important days of Derrick's life and I couldn't be more proud of him. After the past three years and the sleepless nights he's finally graduating from Harvard Law. Oh, only if Papa were here to see him walk across that stage today. I know he's watching Derrick every day and he's more than proud of the man he has become, but today is their day.

In celebration of this day, I invited my family as well as Rose and Bud over for breakfast. I thought it would be a nice idea to have us all here together in our home before heading over to Cambridge for his commencement.

Looking over at the clock I still have an hour before everyone arrives and Derrick should be back from his run any minute. I quickly set out some last minute things and then make my way back to our bedroom to get ready.

I have already laid out my outfit for today along with my jewelry and shoes. Since the main color of Harvard is crimson red, I thought it was fitting to purchase a dress that would match for some school spirit. Beside my dress I have set out Derrick's suit, dress shirt, tie and his graduation gown. As I stare down at our items a tear runs down my cheek.

My heart begins to break as I realize what I have to tell Derrick today. I have wanted to talk to him about this for the past three weeks, but I have a decision to make. I know I should have talked to him about this before today, but it never seemed to be the right time. Now of all days I have to tell him that our lives are about to change. Not only is he graduating from law school, but I too have received an opportunity of a lifetime that I just cannot refuse.

I wipe the tears from my cheeks that are now pouring out of my eyes and head into the bathroom. The bathroom begins to steam up and I enter the shower and hurry to clean myself so that I can get ready before our families come. Today is Derrick's day and I promise not to ruin it until the very last minute. I may be the worst girlfriend in the world after today, but that is a risk I have to take. Chances like this only come once a lifetime.

The bathroom door opens and I can see Derrick through the glass shower doors. He strips his running gear off and pulls down two towels for us setting them on the hooks next to the shower. He slides open the shower door and moves in behind me.

"You don't mind do you?" He asks.

I try to pull myself together. He can't know that I've been crying.

"Of course I don't mind, actually I was hoping you would come in to wash my back."

"Perfect timing then, huh?"

"Yes, you are perfect Derrick."

"Awe Angel, come here. Let me love you."

Derrick turns me to face him, but I can't seem to open my eyes for fear that the tears will pour out and I'll have no choice but to tell him now. He brings his lips to mine and we begin to explore one another in the most sensual way. Derrick nips at my lip and licks his tongue to my ear lobe. He places a kiss to my collar bone and then takes both of my breasts in his hands. Massaging them ever so gently he licks my nipples one at a time till both are pebbled from my arousal. This man's touch does things to my mind and body. I can't get enough of him.

My leg is lifted and placed on the stool within the tile shower. Derrick kneels down in front of me and fits his head between my legs. My body becomes weak and I'm not sure if I'll be able to keep my stance for much longer. Derrick sweeps his arm around my waist to support me while his other hand is slowly inserting two fingers into my aching pussy. He licks at my clit while fingering me until I'm swept away with my orgasm.

"That's it Angel, let it all go."

His words push me to the edge and I'm overwhelmed with the warmth that spreads through my body.

Derrick carefully stands and brings his other arm around to my waist lifting me against the tile wall. I wrap my legs around him as he slides his length between my wet folds. I finally open my eyes and stare into his baby blues. I pump myself up and down his shaft while he bites his lip feeling the rhythm we are creating. The water is spraying down onto our bodies and we're becoming a slippery mix of love and lust. The way he makes me feel is like nothing I ever want to rid myself of….ever.

I can feel myself falling toward another orgasm and Derrick clenches my ass cheeks while lifting me up and down onto him.

"Fuck Chloe you feel so good."

"Derrick."

With a few more strokes up and down his erection we are both falling to the shower floor in a heap of spent energy.

"I love you Chloe."

"I love you too Derrick. Happy graduation day."

We both laugh and try to stand with week limbs. Managing to continue our shower we wash one another and help to rinse any excess soap from our bodies. I follow Derrick out of the shower and into the bedroom. Together we help each other dress. We pay extra special attention to our hands on the other's body. I know today is a special day for him, but for some reason I feel like every look, each touch and all his words have an important meaning behind them.

Something seems different and I hope it's not me feeling insecure about what I need to talk to him about tonight.

DERRICK

I set my alarm a little earlier for today. It isn't everyday you graduate from law school and propose to the love of your life. My mind and body are in desperate need of at least a hard five mile run. I just need to make sure I can get it in before the family comes over for breakfast.

While on my run my thoughts are going in a million directions. There's no doubt in my mind what her answer will be, but still I want to make sure everything about tonight is perfect. I must have gone over this plan a dozen times since I woke this morning. Everything has to be just right.

Rounding the corner into our development I can feel a cheesy grin cross my face. If anyone were to see me right now they would think I'd lost my mind. I hurry into the driveway and type in the combination to the garage. Tossing my running sneakers onto the shelf, I close the door and make my way upstairs to our room.

I can hear the water running in the shower and quickly make my way in to join her. I don't know why, but I ask if it's okay that I join her. I sure as hell am glad I did. Chloe and I have the hottest shower sex ever. I just can't wait till tonight to do it all over again and make love to her as my fiancé.

We help one another dry off and move into the bedroom. Chloe has laid out our clothes for the day and I see that she's wearing a crimson red dress. She's going to look hot as hell wearing this and I'm proud to show her off as my girl. Once she has on her bra, panties and pantyhose I help her put on the dress and pull the zipper up in the back for her. She turns around for me to see her in the full get up and that does it. She just takes my breath away. I can't believe in only a few hours she will be my fiancée.

"You look beautiful Angel." I tell her.

"Thank you Derrick." She says with a blush.

I bring her in for a kiss and then the doorbell rings.

"Great timing." I say with a pout.

Chloe laughs and kisses me on the lips. She puts on her shoes and heads down the hallway. I hear the voices of my parents and figure I better hurry up and get ready.

By the time I make it downstairs the dining room and living room are filled with our families and the smell of breakfast.

"Congrats to the grad!" Charlie shouts and comes over to give me a hug.

"Thanks Charlie." I say returning the tight squeeze.

I continue to make my rounds to the rest of our company giving hugs, kisses and accepting the praise of the family. Today is going to have my nerves tied up in knots. Not only am I accepting a diploma for my Juris Doctorate, but I'm fucking proposing tonight. Both of our families are in on the surprise and I'm hoping they've kept their mouths shut. I want this to be a surprise. I want this night to sweep her off of her feet. I only get one chance at this and I don't want anything to screw it up for us.

I spot Chloe in the kitchen and make my way in to see if I can help her with anything. Pulling her into me, I kiss her on the cheek and can feel her smile.

"Need any help in here Angel?" I ask.

"Nope, we are all set for everyone to start eating. We have plenty of time before we have to leave. Go grab yourself some food and make yourself comfortable. You have a big day ahead of you." She says.

"Thank you for all of this Chloe. You know I appreciate everything you do for me."

"I know love, now go eat." She says and kisses me on the lips.

My girl is absolutely perfect.

After we eat the families pile into their cars and we follow one another to Cambridge. Commencement is set to begin at 11 o'clock and should be wrapped up around 4 o'clock. I know I should be excited for graduation, but really I just want it to be over so that I can spend the rest of the day I have planned for me and Chloe.

During the ceremony I do my best to pay attention to the speakers and the line of students I'm supposed to follow up to the stage. Once I'm in front of the dean and accepting my paper in hand I look out to the crowd and envision Chloe's smiling face. The past three years of me in school have been difficult for both of us, but today is proof that it was all worth it.

I walk around to the area our families are sitting in and receive hugs all around.

"I'm so proud of you Derrick." Mom says.

"Me too." Teresa squeals pulling me in for a big hug.

"Come here stud, I'm so happy for you. It's nice to know we have a lawyer in the family. You know…just in case." Charlie says.

I bypass the rest of the crew and head straight for my girl. Chloe sees me approaching her and brings her arms out to embrace me in a hug. I squeeze her tight and lift her into my arms.

"We did it Angel. Today starts a new life for me and you, one that I promise will make you happy for the rest of our lives."

I continue to hug her while twirling her in my arms.

Bryce and my dad come walking over to me and I give them both a scowl. I don't want to let her go, but I guess I better accept the congrats I'm going to get from our fathers.

"Nice work son, we are all so proud of you." Bryce says shaking my hand and giving me a firm pat on the back.

"He's right Derrick, we're all so proud of you. You know Papa is looking down on you today with tears in his eyes. You made a dream come true just like you told him you would."

"Thanks dad, that means a lot to me." I reply giving him a hug.

I pull Chloe back against my side give her a kiss on the cheek and turn to face our families.

"Thank you all so much for coming today. It has been a crazy journey for Chloe and I, but today makes all of our struggles well worth it. I appreciate you guys so much for being there for us and I couldn't have done it without my family. Now if you don't mind, I have a celebration dinner planned for me and my girl."

Taking Chloe by the hand I escort her out of the auditorium and to my car. I remove my cap and gown and hand it to Chloe to fold up for me. I know better than to try and do it myself. Once she has it perfect, I set it in the backseat and open the passenger side door for her.

My heart is thumping in my chest and I feel like I'm about to pass out. I can do this, I know I can.

Chapter 9

CHLOE

After Derrick's graduation we get into his car and head toward East Boston. He told our families we were off for a celebration dinner which sounds like fun, but I have a lump in my throat and in the pit in my stomach. I don't know how much longer I can keep my secret to myself. I need to tell him and I don't know when will be the right moment.

It probably wasn't the best idea to accept a job offer without talking to him, but my god this really is a chance of a lifetime. I really didn't even see this coming, it just happened so fast.

I'm sitting in my office at the WZDH Channel 7NBC studios in Boston where I've been working for the past two and half years. I'm scheduled to attend the Red Sox vs. Phillies game tonight at 7:30 and trying to get some last minutes edits worked through before I have to leave.

I look up when I hear a knock on my door and my boss Sean is standing there with another person. He introduces me to Traci Roche with ESPN Live out of Los Angeles. I stand from my desk and approach the two of them, my hand extended to greet her with a handshake.

My knees feel weak and my heart is pumping through my chest. Shit, my hands are sweating, I just shook Traci Roche's hand and my fucking hands are sweaty...just great!

"Hi Chloe, it's a sincere pleasure to meet you. We've been watching you for quite some time now and felt it was time to present you with an offer."

"An offer?" I look between Sean and Traci. "I'm sorry. I'm a little confused. What offer?"

Traci looks at Sean and lets out a laugh.

"Yes Chloe. ESPN would like to offer you a sport's analyst position with ESPN Live. You have had quite the career since graduating from NYU and we'd love to have you as a member of our team."

She watches me intently as I walk back over to my desk and take a seat. I think I'm honestly in shock. This stuff doesn't happen to people like me. Derrick and I are just ordinary people that get up go to work, come home and go to bed...well after having really hot sex, then we go to bed.

Oh god what the hell!

"So what do you say Chloe?" She asks taking a seat across from me at my desk.

"Wow! I'm speechless."

"That's a surprise." Sean says with a laugh.

"Did you know about this Sean?" I ask looking him dead in his green eyes.

He runs his hands through his blonde hair and takes a seat next to Traci.

"Well I kind of sent them some stuff about you a few months back. Don't be mad Chloe. I know this is your dream job and you've done such an amazing job here. I just had to help you get your name out there."

"Thanks Sean, really I'm grateful. And thank you Traci for coming all this way to see me. It's all just a bit much to take in. I was just preparing to leave for the game."

"Don't worry about the game. I've got you covered tonight."

It feels like yesterday I was in that room with both Sean and Traci. Who knew so much would have changed in such a short amount of time. I don't know if I made the wrong decision accepting the job, but I have to do this for me. It's my dream and I know Derrick will understand. We will find a way to make it work. It might be hard at first, but we did it before and being apart only made our relationship that much stronger.

The sound of Derrick's voice takes me out of my thoughts.

"We're almost there Angel, just a few more minutes. You okay? You seem quiet since we left the school." He asks and runs his hand up and down my thigh.

I grab onto his hand and smile. Talking right now might just bring me to a fit of tears. I'll tell him after dinner. I can do this.

I look out the window and see that we're pulling into Pier Park. This was one of the places Derrick and I'd go to sit and relax when it was too cold to take out his boat. There are still a lot of crazy people out there that don't mind the cold. It's a beautiful scene to see the other boats out on the water.

My gaze looks toward Derrick and he turns to me. A big grin is on his face.

"What are we doing here Derrick?" I ask.

"You'll see. It's a surprise. Wait here, I'll be right back."

I watch as he gets out of the car and comes over to my side to open the door.

"Such a gentleman."

"Always for you love."

Well if I wasn't in love with this man, I sure would be smitten by now. He takes my hand and pulls me over to a roped off area.

"Derrick, it doesn't look like they want anyone in here." I say trying to pull him back.

"Exactly, we don't want anyone in here to disturb us."

He continues to pull me into a spot where a small white tent is set up. What is this man up to? He turns to look at me and pulls me into his embrace. Placing his lips against mine he gives me a passionate kiss that I know I'll remember forever. He pulls away just enough to look into my eyes.

"Chloe I love you more than anything in this whole world. Today is the start of a beautiful future for us and I wanted to make this night perfect. First we're going to have dinner here at Pier Park and later I'm taking you to a very special place."

I'm in awe of him in this moment. I can barely speak. I just nod my head and follow him into the white tent.

DERRICK

The entire ride over to Pier Park my heart is beating so hard I fear that Chloe can hear it. She has been so quiet since we left the graduation. I hope she is feeling alright and nothing happened to upset her. It would kill me if she was in a bad mood for tonight. I want everything to be perfect. This is a night she will remember for the rest of our lives.

I look over at her and she has her hands twisted up into her lap and she seems like she's off in deep thought. I need to break the silence before I pull into the parking lot.

"We're almost there angel, just a few more minutes. You okay? You seem to be pretty quiet since we left the school."

Instead of responding she smiles and nods her head. Damn it to hell! I'll do just about anything to ensure this night makes her happy. And it all starts right now.

I plaster a huge grin on my face and tell her to wait while I come around to open her door.

I open the door for her and take her hand. I'm so fucking nervous I can't even remember if I have the damn ring. I put my hand in my pocket and fish around till I feel the little bag mom gave me to put it in. Phew, that's the last thing I need to stress about tonight.

We walk toward the center of the park where a small white tent has been set up for a romantic dinner. It took just about all my connections in Boston to pull this shit together and from the looks of it they all did a great job.

Chloe tugs on my arm and says we shouldn't go through the ropes. I laugh to myself, oh dear Chloe just wait. I'm about to knock your socks off.

I tell her it's okay and pull her to follow me.

When we reach the outside of the white tent I pull her in close to me. She really is one of the most important people in my life and this night is going to be one to tell our grandkids about.

As we enter the tent I hear her gasp. I turn to face her and I see her hand is pressed over her mouth and tears are streaming down her cheeks. I pull her into me and kiss her forehead. She begins to tremble in my arms and I run my hand up and down her back to soothe her.

"Oh my god Derrick, this is beautiful. You did this for us? How did you do this? I mean wow!" She says wiping the tears from her face and looking around the inside of the tent.

I must say the guys did a fucking fantastic job. The walls of the tent are trimmed in white lights. There are red roses scattered all along the wooden floor and a table is set for two in the middle. Soft music is playing in the back corner and there are candles surrounding a small dance floor.

"I wanted tonight to be special for us. We have a lot to celebrate Chloe." I tell her putting a fallen piece of hair behind her ear.

"It's beautiful, its amazing Derrick. Thank you."

"You don't have to thank me Angel. Come let's sit down and eat. Then we can do some dancing before we leave."

Chloe follows me over to the table and I pull out her seat. She sits and I help get her comfortable. I take my own seat and look across the table. She's taking it all in looking around the small room set up here in the middle of Pier Park. It's the most romantic moment and I'm so glad it's us in here together.

She looks up at me with her big brown eyes and gives me that killer smile. I return the smile and grab her hand giving it a kiss.

"Today has been absolutely one of the best days of my life Chloe. You and I really have been through just about everything and I'm so glad that we have made it to this point."

"Me too Derrick. I really am so proud of you for doing all this. You have accomplished every goal you've ever set for yourself. You inspire me to do the same."

"I did it all because I want us to have a great life together. With you by my side I know that will happen."

"I know." She replies

"Well come on let's eat before our dinner gets cold."

"It smells amazing."

I lift the silver domes off of the plates and we begin to dig in to our food. It tastes so good and I'm starving. As much as I want to move onto the next destination of our evening I can't help but enjoy this moment watching Chloe. She's the most beautiful woman in the world. Her long dark hair is falling in waves to her mid back. The crimson red dress she's wearing shows her amazing curves and when she looks at me with those eyes… she just takes my breath away.

"Dinner was wonderful Derrick." She says tossing her linen napkin onto her plate.

"Oh do you hear that?" I ask.

"Hear what." She says looking around the tent.

"I think they are playing our song."

She looks over to where the music is set up and she stares, like that will help her hear better.

I stand alongside the table next to her and extend my hand.

"May I have this dance?" I ask.

"I can't believe this night Derrick, it's our song."

"It sure is Angel. Come on let's dance to it."

I walk her over to the small dance floor area and swing her around in my arms. As we dance to our song, Lucky by Jason Mraz and Colbie Caillat, I envision what it will be like to dance with her to this song on our wedding day. I pull her in closer to me so that I can feel her heart beating against mine. This day has been absolutely perfect and there's just one more thing I need to do. I pull away from her just enough so that I can look into her eyes again.

"You're so beautiful to me Chloe." I tell her and kiss her lips ever so softly.

"I love you so much Derrick. No matter what we've been through we always make it work. You make us work. I love you."

She kisses me back but instead of a soft kiss she kisses me fiercely. I feel tears coming down our cheeks and I pull away.

"Don't cry Angel. This is all for you. Everything I do is for you so that our future is perfect. Come on we have one last surprise for the night."

Chloe holds onto my arm and follows me through the tent and out into the park toward my car.

We're about fifteen minutes away from our next destination and I'm about as antsy as a four-year-old at an ice cream shop waiting for his treat. My left leg is twitching and I'm beginning to get a headache from clenching my teeth.

I look over to Chloe and she's resting her head back against the seat with her eyes shut. This is perfect; she won't notice where we are until we're parked right out and in front of it.

After exactly fifteen minutes I pull into our final stop for tonight.

"Chloe love, we're here." I say rubbing her thigh.

"Oh no, sorry Derrick I must have dozed off."

"No worries Angel let me come around and get the door for you."

When I open the door for her she stands up and looks around.

"Why are we…?"

I quickly put my finger to her lips and guide her to the side of the house. We walk hand in hand until I feel her stop.

"Oh. My. God. Derrick!" She shouts.

She kind of throws me off guard and for a moment I'm looking at her and back to our spot. I quickly gather my bearings and continue to walk toward our tree. Teresa, mom and Charlie did a fucking amazing job. The tree has tiki torches lit around the outside and they've sectioned off branches so that there's a wide opening for us to walk into. Inside of the weeping willow tree is our bench with a table filled with candles and roses.

I walk us inside of the tree and wait for the music to start. Moments later the melody starts and I pull her into an embrace. I hold her tightly as her body shakes against mine. In a few seconds I realize it's not her body trembling but my own. I need to do this now before I blow it with an anxiety attack.

Pulling slightly away from her I rub my thumb along her lower lip and sweep away the tears that are now falling from her eyes.

"Derrick this entire day has been one surprise after another. This is your day and you're doing so much for me."

I step back from her and take her hands in mine. Looking into her eyes I know it's time.

"Chloe I can't tell you enough how special you are to me, or how much I love you. For the past eight years you have been my soul mate, the one I find peace with. You're my forever Chloe and today is just the beginning of great things to come for us. Without you in my life things would be empty. You honestly make me who I am. I'm a better man because of you."

My fucking hands are shaking so bad. I remove my hand from hers and reach into my pocket. I remove the ring from the bag and have it in my hand. I look at her and start to get down on one knee.

"Chloe……"

"No wait Derrick stop. You can't…I'm sorry, but I have to tell you something before you say anything else."

My heart stops. I am blind by fear. What the hell would she have to tell me that would make her stop me from proposing?

Chapter 10

CHLOE

Oh no….no…this can't be happening. Everything he has done today was all for this. Oh my God he's going to propose and I haven't told him I'm leaving for LA in a few weeks. My body is numb, my heart has stopped beating and my hands are getting sweaty. I can barely breathe as I see him reaching in his pocket. This has been the perfect day leading up to this moment. He has planned this amazingly romantic day for me and he's going to propose under our tree.

God Chloe, you're such a bitch for doing this to him. I have to stop him before he goes any further.

I watch as he begins to get down on one knee and he says my name. I quickly put my finger to his lips to stop him before he says anything more. I'm about to break his heart and all for my own selfish needs.

"No wait. Derrick stop. You can't…I'm sorry, but I have to tell you something before you say anything else."

His body slouches to the ground and from his knees he's now sitting on his ass. The pain of what I've just done courses through my body and I'm so scared to speak. Once I tell him the path I have chosen our lives will be changed forever. There is no going back on this now.

"I'm sorry Derrick. Today has been absolutely wonderful and you have no idea how special you have made me feel. I just…I need to tell you something and it may change the way you feel and wanting to ask me those words."

Sitting down in the grass next to him I take his hands in mine. He turns his face to look at me and confusion is spread across his eyes.

"I've wanted to tell you this for the past few weeks, well actually the past month or so. The timing just never felt right and now it's almost as if it's too late."

He pulls his hands from mine and moves to stand. Grabbing for my hands he pulls me up and leads me to our bench. We sit in silence for what feels like forever and then he lifts me into his lap. He rubs up and down my back to comfort me. I'm about to rip apart his night and he's soothing me. Derrick is the most remarkable man I've ever known.

"Chloe, I have no clue what is happening right now. I feel numb. It's like someone ripped out my heart and I don't even know what you have to tell me yet. I planned this perfect day, this romantic night. I was going to propose to you Chloe. We were going to start our new lives together…tonight. And you stopped me, why did you stop me?"

I pull his face toward mine and kiss him. I want so badly to make him feel loved and like this will be okay. He pulls away from the kiss and stares at me with his baby blue eyes.

"Please tell me Chloe, I have to know what is going on. Did I do something wrong?"

"Oh no Derrick. You've done nothing wrong. This is harder now than I ever thought it would be."

"Are you breaking up with me?" He asks in a whisper.

"No…please no, don't think that. I love you so much Derrick. It's just…ugh!" I shout and stand to walk pacing the inner circle of the tree branches.

A few moments pass and Derrick comes over to me pulling me into his embrace. Tears prick at the back of my eyelids and as soon as I open them to look at him the dam bursts and tears are flooding my vision.

"Whatever it is tell me. We will get through it together. As long as you love me and I love you we can make it work."

"You're too good to me Derrick, I love you so much."

"I know, now let's go sit so you can tell me why you stopped me from asking you to marry me."

We sit back down on the bench and Derrick pulls my face into his hands. He lightly kisses my lips and tells me everything will be okay. I feel better knowing he's willing to support me even though I'm about to crush him.

"Derrick…there's no easy way to put this. I'm leaving for Los Angeles."

I look up into his eyes and his face is flushed with fear. I grip onto his hands. I can feel him start to shake.

"What do you mean you're leaving for Los Angeles? Like for a trip, a vacation, for what Chloe?" He asks staring into my eyes.

I can barely speak as the tears fall from my eyes.

"I'm sorry Derrick, I couldn't say no. This is my dream."

"Chloe, I'm so fucking confused right now and to tell you the truth I'm getting pissed off. What the hell do you mean you're leaving for LA? What fucking dream are you talking about?"

Obviously Derrick is beyond pissed at me and I can't really blame him. I move back from him so that I'm not touching him. It's hard enough to explain this without the warmth of his touch consuming my body.

"A few months ago Sean came into my office with a member of ESPN Live's crew. It was Traci Roche. She came all the way to Boston to let me know that they've been watching my career and felt it was time to offer me a position as an analyst on ESPN. Derrick, I'm so sorry I didn't tell you sooner. I just didn't know what to do. They called me Monday and told me they needed me to be out there the beginning of June. I had to give them an answer."

"And let me guess you told them yes. That is what this is all about. You're telling your boyfriend that you made a decision to pick up and move across country without even talking to me? How could you Chloe? Fuck your damn dreams for a fucking minute. Did you even consider what would happen to us with the choices you were making? No, because you never think of anyone but yourself. God damn it Chloe, I was going to fucking propose to you. I wanted to ask you to marry me and be with me forever. And because you didn't have the decency to talk to me about this months ago…we…its…FUCK Chloe!"

Derrick gets up from the bench and begins to pace the same path through the inner branches as I was a few minutes ago.

"I'm sorry Derrick." I say with tears still pouring from my eyes.

"Sorry doesn't cut it this time Chloe. I can't do this right now. I'm going home to think. I suggest you stay here for the night."

He begins to walk out of the branches when he turns and looks at me. His eyes are red and swollen from crying. His hair is a styled mess from running his hands through it in fury.

"Don't think about calling me tonight either Chloe. I can't deal with you tonight. I want to be alone. Got it?"

I can't speak. He hates me. I just nod my head and turn my back. I can't watch him walk away like this.

DERRICK

I can't believe this is happening. What the fuck Chloe? I slam my hand down on the steering wheel. I'm so angry right now I don't know what I want to do with this information. How could she make a decision like this without even talking to me? Yeah, okay, I get that this is her dream. But what the fuck, aren't I a part of her life? I thought we were more of a pair than this.

God damn! Motherfucking! Piss ant! Fucktard! Stupid shit! Just fucking fucktasitic! Ugh! I scream in my car.

I reach into my pocket and pull out her ring. Glancing down at it I begin to cry. Thankfully I'm pulling into our driveway and I throw the car into park and turn off the ignition. I settle my head against the steering wheel and bang on it a few times, hoping this is just a really bad nightmare.

But then I realize it isn't a nightmare at all, its reality and I just lost the love of my life.

I pull myself out of my car and close the garage door. Making my way into the house I head down to the basement into my man cave. I need to find something to numb this pain so I look through the liquor cabinet. I spot a bottle of whiskey and grab a glass. I set her ring on the bar. I reach in the freezer and toss in two ice cubes while filing the glass to the top. This should do the trick. I climb onto the couch, kick off my shoes and gulp down my poison. Before I know it the glass is empty and I pass out.

Voices? Do I hear voices? I sit up and grab my head. What the fuck? I look around the room and see the bottle of whiskey and a glass sitting on the table. I hear voices and footsteps coming down into the basement. Maybe if I hide they'll go away. Ugh, my head is killing me. I need aspirin like yesterday.

"Derrick? You down here?"

What the hell is Charlie doing here?

"Derrick Mason Peters! We know you're here your car is in the garage."

Oh damn it to hell she's here with my mom. I need to get my ass up before they come in here and pull me out of the man cave. Walking over to the door three women storm in after me and I fall back into the couch.

"Thank god we found him!" My mom shrieks.

"Mom, come on, not so loud. Where the hell else would I be? This is my house."

"Yes I know this is your house dear, but we've all been calling you since you walked out on Chloe last night. We were worried sick about you."

"Well I'm here and as you can see I'm perfectly fine."

"You don't look fine to me. You want to talk about it?" Charlie asks.

"Come on ladies we can see he is okay, why don't we go upstairs and make him something to eat." Teresa says pulling the others by their arms.

"You guys go ahead. I'm going to stay down here and talk with him." Charlie says pulling her arm from her mom's grasp.

"Okay honey. You two meet us in the kitchen in fifteen minutes."

I watch as their conversation takes place right in front of me like I'm not even here. Mom and Teresa walk out of the room closing the door and Charlie hops on the couch next to me.

"So you freaked, huh?"

"Do you know what really happened Charlie or are you just taking Chloe's word for it?"

"Look Derrick the news of LA was a surprise to all of us, no one saw this coming. If I knew I swear I would have told you."

"I know you would have Charlie. You're a great friend you know that?"

"Hell yeah I do. Who else would put up with all you and Chloe's drama if I wasn't around?"

"I guess I overreacted and said some stuff that I didn't mean to. I'm sure she is just as upset over this as I'm, right?"

"Derrick she is beside herself right now. I don't think moving away is the best thing, I kind of hate it too, but this is all she has ever dreamed about you know. I just wish she could land that kind of job here in Boston."

"Me too Charlie, me too. So what's next? Do we stay together? Do we break up? I'm so confused."

"I bet you are. I would be. One thing is for certain Derrick. You both love each other more than anything. I think you need to talk to her and figure out what is best for both of you. She's going whether you and I like it or not."

"I know. I'm proud of her. It just sucks. I'm going to go grab a shower and give her a call. Tell our moms I'll grab some breakfast on the way out."

I get up to walk out of the room and turn to face Charlie.

"Thanks for everything Charlie. You're always there for us."

I continue up to me and Chloe's room. As much as I hate what just happened last night, I can't give up on what we have. I need to let her know that we will make this work. We have to make this work…no matter what.

Chapter 11
August 2012

CHLOE

It's been a rough few months to say the least. Since living in New York I never spent this much time away from my family or Derrick for that matter. I do my best to keep busy with work and socialize with some friends, but my heart still hurts. I miss him.

Now here I am living in Los Angeles working as an ESPN sports analyst and living my dream job. Things worked out well for me in the career sector of my life, it just sucks that I'm thousands of miles away from my true love, Derrick.

After the night he was about to propose I didn't think we were going to make it as a couple. Well actually that's a lie. I knew we would make it, but it was going to be hard. Derrick and I talked about the chance of me moving to the west coast when we were in college, but then again that was years ago and neither of us thought my pipe dream would come true.

Then it happened. I was offered my dream job. Everything I'd ever wanted was right in front of me, but I had to choose.

The morning after he walked away from me I woke up feeling like the world was about to end. My head was pounding, my eyes hurt and it felt like my chest was split in two. Ugh! I hate to think back to that day.

"Hey sleepy head how are you feeling?" Dad asks.

"Fine." I reply. "Where is everyone?"

"They went over to the house to check on Derrick. You okay sweetie?"

"I'm good Daddy, thanks. I think I'm just going to take a shower and relax downstairs for a bit. Let mom know I'm down there when she gets back."

"Okay Chloe, I'll be outside if you need me."

I made my way downstairs and took a hot shower. The feel of the water pricking my skin hurt at first, but after awhile it started to numb the pain. I just wish it could have taken the pain away in my chest. Shortly after the water started to cool I dried off, got dressed and laid down on the couch.

I closed my eyes for what felt like a brief moment and was woken up by warm arms pulling me into an embrace. I could smell his cologne and body wash, it was Derrick. I didn't want to open my eyes for fear that I was dreaming, but I took the chance and there he was.

"What are you doing here? I thought you didn't want to see me ever again."

"Angel, I'm sorry. I was so upset and said some awful things to you last night. Please forgive me."

"Derrick I'm the one that should be sorry. I ruined everything."

He pulled me away from him so that we were facing each other. Wiping away my tears he kissed my lips.

I missed him so much in only a short amount of time.

"I don't like the idea of you living on the other side of the country Chloe. I won't lie about that." He says running his hands through my hair.

Looking into his eyes I can see the pain and hurt.

"We'll get through this. I promise." I tell him pulling us closer together. I need him and I need his touch to reassure me we will really be okay.

I let out a deep sigh at the memories and try to regain my composure. Things have been okay between Derrick and me since I left. We talk at least once a day and Skype every night before bed. I know everything happens for a reason and we're strong together as a couple.

Walking toward the gate I smile, this week is going to be fun and exciting. My mom and dad are flying in today and I have a jam packed week of activities for us to do. I want them to see why I love LA so much and know that I'm truly happy with the decisions I've made.

I can see my dad come through the tunnel first. Daddy really is quite the handsome man at 56. He is 6'4", dark hair and eyes with a distinct mustache that drives me crazy. Coming up behind him I can see my mom. She too is attractive. Though mom is much shorter than dad, she still stands tall at about 5'7" with long dark hair, deep brown eyes and a smile that can go on for miles. I walk quickly over to them and dad grabs me up in a bear hug. As he puts my feet to the ground, mom comes over and gives me a warm hug. I feel loved and protected now that the two of them are here.

Out of nowhere two hands come around my face covering my eyes. I squeal with nervousness and pry the hands off of my face. Turning around to see who would do such a thing, I spot my little sister Char.

Holy shit! What a great surprise.

"What is going on here? Am I being punk'd?"

"No you are not being punk'd loser, you're way not famous enough for that." She says.

"Come on girls; let's move this act of affection away from the gate. You two are going to get us kicked out of the damn airport." Dad tells us in a stern tone.

Char and I finally break free from our embrace and I walk the four of us out of the airport and out to the parking lot where my car is waiting.

I take them straight to my apartment to get settled in and then plan on going out for a nice dinner welcoming my family to LA.

Curling up on the couch I look toward Char and ask, "So Char tell me all about this hot roommate Derrick has staying with him. Derrick said Riley has quite the crush on you. Spill it girl."

"Wait, what? Char you just said there was nothing going on between you two." Daddy says in an odd tone.

Char seriously looks like she is about to spew so I figure I'll lay off the Riley topic for now. I can dig in later when it's just the two of us.

Spending this week with my family has been exactly what I've needed since moving out here. The best part so far was bringing them down to the studio and introducing them to some of the analysts. To me they are just normal people, but to everyone else I suppose we're famous. Daddy nearly passed out when Erika Anderson walked in while I was giving the grand tour. Talk about a fan moment.

Since today is their last day here I set up an appointment for Char and me at the salon and sent mom and dad off on a tourist mission. I want to spend some time talking to my sister about her and this Riley guy. I have a sneaky suspicion that she is holding back because of her last relationship and I want my sister to find her happiness.

While we're waiting in the whirlpool to get our massages I look over at her.

"Thanks so much for doing this with me today Char." It really is great to have her here with me in LA and having a day to just relax and bond.

She refuses to be the one that is being thanked, she feels this day is a treat and she should be thanking me. Honestly I'm just glad to be here with her.

"So tell me why you came out here to see me." I ask.

She plays it off as if it's no big deal that she dropped everything to come out here, but I know her better than that.

"Chloe?" She looks over at me and a tear trickles down her face.

"Yeah, sweetie?" I reply putting my hand on her arm and slowly start to brush back and forth in a comforting rhythm.

"I don't think...I don't know."

"Look I know what Marc did to you was awful, no one deserves to be lied to and cheated on the way he did to you. You have to remember that none of it was your fault. He was a complete jackass and was unhappy with himself in many ways. You two were so wrong for each other from the start, but you always saw the good in him. You always see the good in everyone. That is why we all love you so much sweetie."

"I just don't think I can ever love again. Marc was my first everything and it just seemed to all line up until he got caught. I know I need to move past it all, but I can't."

"You can and you will. Char you're absolutely gorgeous, have the body I would kill for, and deserve to be happy. I'm quite certain this Riley fellow is just as smitten with you as you are with him. Just admit it girl."

My poor sister lacks confidence in the relationship department, but I have a good feeling that now when she goes home she is going to start anew. I'm proud of the woman she has become and the future she is building for herself. She deserves to be happy.

DERRICK

I caved. As much as I hated the fact that Chloe was going to move across country I let her do it. I mean, what kind of boyfriend would I be to hold her back from her dreams? We promised each other that we would talk everyday and once our schedules were set we would visit. And we pretty much have done just that. She has only been gone a few months, but we still talk and text each day and Skype before bed. I love seeing and hearing her voice, but it's not the same as her being here and in my arms. Thanksgiving vacation can't come soon enough. I'll have to fight our families to spend time with her. I have a pretty good feeling I'll win that battle.

Things have gotten really busy at Jax & Paige and I want to do my best to prove my worth to the senior partners. I enjoy what I do and I must say I'm getting pretty good at it. My win to loss case ratio is the best of the junior partners and according to some of the big guys I have a promising career ahead of me. If it weren't for this work load, I think I'd go insane. Thankfully in my spare time I'm working on our house and I now have a roommate, Riley and his dog Manny, to keep me company…well sometimes.

Not only do I have the drama of my relationship with Chloe to worry about, but my new roommate Riley is crushing on Chloe's sister and my best friend Charlie. I can't say that it would be a bad thing for them to hook up. They're both really great people and have a lot in common. It's just that lately he's acting like a chick moping about since Charlie pushed him away. Man o man, grow a pair and fight for her already.

Today Riley starts his new job at Taylor & Sons Contracting so being the nice guy I am I think I'll make him some coffee to start the day. I can hear Manny's paws coming down the hardwood steps and run straight for the sliding glass door. I make my way over and let him out. Riley turns into the kitchen and sees the cup of coffee sitting on the table. He gives me a look and I laugh.

"Hey man, all set for your big day at work? I'm so excited for you that I got up early and wanted to make you breakfast. Before you open your trash mouth, no I'm not a bitch; I'm a very good friend who wants you to have an even better day."

"Awe shucks thanks honey, I didn't know you felt that way about me. At least someone loves me."

He sits down at the table with a pout on his face. Damn this guy looks pitiful.

"Come on man, everything happens for a reason, right? Look at it this way, if you two are meant to be she'll come back. Just be patient with her. She's had a shitty relationship past and the last asshole did a number on her."

"I get that Derrick, I do. She just won't even give us a chance. I feel like a chick moping around, but she's gotten to me and in like no time at all."

"Those Taylor girls are something Riley. I've been with Chloe for years and in that time we've had great times and times that have really sucked. But I believe we're meant to be. No matter what life throws at us, we still get by."

"Yeah I guess you're right. Well I'm going to go put my balls back on and get ready for work. Thanks for the coffee and the pep talk bro. It helps to have a friend like you around."

I tried to do my best to lift the guy's spirits, whether it worked or not I don't know. Finishing up my breakfast I clean up my mess and head upstairs to take a shower. Here's to another week, got to love Mondays.

The week goes by damn fast and I love the fact that each week brings me closer to Chloe's visit for Thanksgiving. We talked a little less this week with her parents and sister in LA, but I know we'll get back to normal next week.

A big topic of conversation for us has been Riley and Charlie. It makes me laugh that I'm the one getting involved in Charlie's romantic drama rather than her dealing with the issues of Chloe and me. I've told Chloe that Riley is pretty down about the way things ended with Charlie before she left for LA and Chloe agrees that Charlie is feeling the same way. To help these two love birds get their act together, Chloe and I have concocted a plan.

All I have to do is let Riley in on the details of tonight and watch the sparks fly. He just needs to get his hung-over ass out of bed. Then I can tell him the details of what he's supposed to do.

When he finally makes his way downstairs, I start his day off the best way I can…with a loud voice of course.

"Hey roomy!" I scream as he passes by me heading to the fridge.

"Shut up asshole. Can't you see I'm in pain here?" He says laying his head down on the counter.

"Look I warned you that those guys from work were trouble. They got to you just like they wanted to and now you have to pay for it all weekend." I say with a belly laugh.

He gives me a killer stare and I know his head has to be hurting from last night's drinking fest with the guys.

"So what's on the agenda for you today?" He asks.

"Well if you must know I'm going to head on over to Charlie's in a bit. Chloe finally scheduled the movers to come and get the last of her things. Since Charlie doesn't fly in till later I said I'd go over and lend a hand."

"Hmm, how nice of you." He says in a sarcastic tone.

"So you want me to let you in on a little secret?" I ask.

At this point I'm so excited for the surprise they're in for, I am almost giddy….almost.

"I don't know, do I?" He replies.

"Well let me just say that it would be cool if you were to be at Charlie's apartment around 6:30 tonight. I would also suggest having a bouquet of wildflowers and take out from the Chinese place down from her apartment warm and ready to eat." He pats me on the back and walks out of the house.

With that I grab my wallet and keys and head out the garage door to my car. Let's see what he makes of that bit of information. I just hope he isn't too hung-over and forgets what I just said. Chloe will kill me.

Who knew Chloe and I would become matchmakers, not I.

Chapter 12
December 2012

CHLOE

While rushing around my apartment I check and double check that everything is perfect before my guests arrive. Okay mental check list go…apartment clean and spotless…check, bedrooms have clean sheets and fresh towels in the bathrooms…check, decorations up and lights on…check, dinner in oven and delicious smells wafting through the air…check, I'm dressed and wearing shoes…check, and lastly Chloe has lost her mind…check, check, check.

I guess I'm just a little excited for Derrick, Char, and Riley to spend the next few days with me in LA. Going back to Boston for Thanksgiving was great, but I hate that I couldn't make it home for Christmas. Just thinking my boyfriend and sister would be here a few days after the holiday helped to ease the pain, but it was still my first Christmas away from family.

My apartment is decorated in the Christmas spirit and I have packages covering the hardwood floors surrounding an eight foot Christmas tree. Hell, just because I wasn't with them on Christmas day doesn't mean we can't celebrate it all over again together here in Los Angeles.

I have a turkey in the oven and even attempted to make mom's filling, sweet potatoes, and apple pie for dessert. The three of them should be here any minute and I'm more than anxious to be spending this week showing Char and Riley my town and then having the week after for just me and Derrick.

My life is completely free the next two weeks so that I can spend every minute with my favorite two people…well and Riley. He's slowly earning the right to be added to my favorites group.

When I met Riley in November I was cautious about his intentions with my sister. I mean come on, who meets someone, falls in love in like a month and then looks into buying a house together a few months later. I was kind of worried that he may be a psychopath. But the minute I saw him I could tell he made my sister happier than I've ever seen her. Char and Riley have a connection similar to Derrick and I. It makes me so happy knowing that she is being taken care of and her world is finally filled with love.

The two love birds did buy a house and lucky for Derrick it's right down the street from ours. Oh god…ours. A sudden feeling of regret fills up my heart and I go back to wondering if I made the right decision to move here to LA.

Buzz, Buzz, Buzz

Shit! I pull myself out of my fog and run over to the speaker on the wall. I push the button and hear Edward's voice coming though the intercom.

"Ms. Chloe, you have three guests in the lobby waiting for you."

"Great Edward, send them up. Thank you." I say in a cheery tone.

I run my fingers through my long dark waves and then press my hands down onto my skirt to remove any wrinkles. I take in a deep breath and adjust my attitude back to happiness and excitement. I'm not going to let any thoughts of regret ruin this trip.

The doorbell rings and I run down the hallway knowing that the love of my life is standing on the other side. I can do this, we can make this work. A few thousand miles are not going to destroy what we have both have worked so hard to achieve.

Come on Chloe, pull your shit together. I take a deep breath in and let it all out. Reaching for the door knob and pulling the door open I put a big smile on my face.

My god there he is. This gorgeous man stands tall at 6'2 wearing dark jeans, a button down white dress shirt and looking absolutely perfect.

I'm in like stun mode and can't move. I'm at a loss for words at the sight of him. A slight smile forms at his lips and his baby blue eyes sparkle with love.

"Chloe I've missed you so much." He says.

Before I can utter a syllable he drops the bags in his hands and scoops me up in his arms. He walks me into my apartment and twirls me around in a circle while peppering kisses along my jaw and then smashing his mouth to mine. I'm truly swept away in the moment and absorbing the feel of my boyfriend. The warmth begins to spread all over my body and any doubt I ever had about us being apart is washed away. I love Derrick Peters and nothing will ever stop my feelings for him.

The sounds of a throat clearing and whistling pulls me back from my Derrick love coma and he slowly sets my feet back down onto the hard floors.

"Good god Chloe I hope you don't expect that kind of greeting from me, at least not in front of Char." Riley says.

"You better not even think about it Riley. The only body your arms get to hold is mine and the only lips you can touch are mine." Char says swatting Riley across the back.

"You two really are too cute together, it's kind of sickening." I laugh.

"Oh my god Chloe like you should talk. For a moment there I felt like I was in a movie the way you two greeted one another. Talk about making me puke." Char replies.

"Come on babe, why don't we grab all the bags and our luggage while these two catch up." Riley suggests to Char.

"Okay Riley, anything you say." Char whispers and then kisses him on the lips.

"Derrick how about I show you to our room so you can make yourself more comfortable." I say starring in his eyes.

"I think that sounds great Angel. Guys we'll be back out in an hour." He says with a laugh and smacking me on the ass.

I missed him more than I ever thought was possible. Everything about him makes me want to pack up and move back home to just be near him. But I can't, that will never happen.

DERRICK

This is my first time coming out to visit Chloe in Los Angeles since she moved last summer. This is where her life is now and the place she has made her home. I'm happy to be spending the next two weeks with her. I want to know more about the things she does here and create memories that will last even after I'm back home in Boston.

"Are you doing okay Derrick?" Charlie asks.

"Yeah, why you ask?" I reply.

"I don't know you just seem off. I mean I'm not a fan of flying either, but ever since we picked you up this morning you just seem quiet."

"I'm okay, just been doing a lot of thinking I guess. Spending the next few weeks with Chloe is definitely needed. I miss her so much and can't wait to be near her again."

"Well Romeo anytime you need us to take a hike just give me the look. Riley and I can go be tourists while the happy couple gets acquainted again."

"Thanks Charlie, I appreciate it."

"Okay good, now snap out of the moody attitude and let's play some cards."

For the rest of our flight Charlie does a good job keeping my mind distracted with cards, a word find and even a little thumb wrestling challenge. I don't know how Riley deals with living with this girl every day. She needs to constantly be doing something to keep herself entertained.

Once the plane lands we walk through the airport find our bags and get our rental car. Being that I'm off in daze Riley chooses to drive and Charlie calls co-pilot. During the half hour drive to Chloe's place I watch as we pass everything that is now home to my girl. This is where she lives, works and will has been creating her future. How the hell will I ever be a part of this? I don't know if it's possible to live this far apart from the one person I love with all my heart knowing that our futures will never be within the same zip code.

Riley pulls the car into the parking garage and I sense them both getting out of the car. I need to get myself out of this funk and fast. I don't want Chloe to know I'm having these thoughts, it could ruin our trip. No even worse, it could ruin everything we have worked so hard to accomplish.

I help Riley and Charlie grab our luggage and bags and head toward the building's lobby. Charlie announces to the gentleman at the desk that we're here to see Chloe Taylor and within a few moments we're on our way up to her place.

A feeling of nervousness takes over and I can't understand why I am anxious to see my girl. It's been a few months since we've been together, but my heart knows we need some time together. That will help me figure out what our next step is moving toward the future.

I stand in front of her door and ring the door bell. I can hear her heels clicking on a tile floor and then the door swings open.

My whole world just stopped. There she stands. My beautiful girl is right here in front of me and all I can do is smile.

"My god Chloe I've missed you so much." I tell her.

I can't waste another second. I need to have her in my arms. Dropping everything in my arms I walk through the doorway and scoop her up in my arms. My lips immediately go to her neck and jaw. I leave a trail of kisses all over her smooth skin. Her smell has me intoxicated and I can feel the warmth of our bodies getting hotter and hotter the longer she is in my grasp. I put my mouth up to hers and kiss her like it's the last time I'll ever see her. God I can't stand this distance between us. Her lips part and I take advantage of the moment by entering her mouth with my tongue. She doesn't hesitate and kisses me back just as passionately.

Riley and Charlie are still standing in the doorway as I spin Chloe in circles continuing to embrace her with all that I have. I guess they get tired of the show, because they start clearing their throats and making whistling noises. Ending our moment I put Chloe's feet back on the floor and allow Riley and Charlie the chance to say hello as well.

Being the jackass Riley is he offers to give Chloe a greeting like mine when Charlie isn't around. Yeah right like hell he will. Still, my good friend offers to get things settled while Chloe shows me to our room. I sure as hell will not argue with getting her in a room alone so I swat her on the ass and follow her lead. Once in the bedroom I take a look around at my surroundings. Her room is decorated just like she started decorating our place back in Boston. It is beautiful yet simple at the same time. The walls are a light grey with blue curtains and darker grey and blue bedding on a queen size sleigh bed. She has a desk, dresser and night stand all in black that match the bed. She just stands there watching me take it all in. I walk over to the desk and see a few picture frames lined up all with photos of me, her and Char.

"I'm so glad you're here." She whispers in my ear while running her hands along my back.

"Me too Chloe, you have no idea how much I missed you." I say turning so that our bodies are facing each other.

"Oh I think I do." She says as she places her soft lips to mine.

I wrap my arms around her holding her in a tight embrace while kissing her more deeply. The feeling of our bodies touching and her mouth on mine has me on fire. There's always a feeling of warmth when I'm around her, but in this moment I'm in flames.

"Damn it Chloe I want to undress you and keep you in this room for the rest of the day." I groan through clenched teeth.

"Oh my God Derrick, if you keep doing that I don't know if I'll ever want to leave this room." She says.

Ever so lightly I continue to rain kisses along her jaw, down her neck and grasping her tits through the fabric of her dress. I'm addicted to this beautiful angel and I've been starved for too long.

"Derrick?" She moans.

"Yes love." I reply.

"As much as I want to strip you of your clothes and take you in my mouth, we have two other people out there and a feast in the oven."

"Fuck Chloe, did you have to say the first part?" I ask.

Pushing away from each other we stare at the lust filled in both our faces and then break into a fit of laughter.

"Okay I'll make a deal with you. Let me take a quick shower and then I'll meet you out there for dinner. We'll spend some time with Charlie and Riley, maybe even exchange some presents, and then I get you all to myself." I tell her.

"I love the way you think Derrick. Get cooled off and I'll see you in the living room in a few minutes."

With that she straightens out her dress, runs her fingers through her hair, and checks her make up in the mirror. She turns blowing me a kiss and then heads out of her bedroom.

Oh yes, that fine ass is all mine and no one is going to stop me from making love to Chloe all night long.

Chapter 13

CHLOE

After the hot make out session with Derrick, I attempt to pull my hormones back together and head out to the kitchen. Char and Riley must still be in the guest room because it's quiet out here. Making my way into the kitchen I open the oven door to check on dinner. Everything looks good to me and should be done within the next fifteen minutes. With just enough time I set the table and pour each of us a glass of white wine.

"You don't have to give Riley any wine, he won't drink it." Char says coming into the dining room.

"Okay, good more for me." I say picking up the glass and downing the few sips I had already poured.

Char laughs at me and shakes her head.

"So how does it feel to have him here?" She asks.

"It's great. I miss him so much and having you all here for New Year's is going to be amazing. There are so many things I have planned for us too."

"I bet you do little miss planner."

"Don't make fun of me. Life is so much simpler when you live by a schedule."

"Yeah okay Chloe. So what's good for dinner?"

"I'm so nervous. I tried to make some of mom's recipes so fingers are crossed it all tastes good."

"Well if it tastes as good as it smells I think we're all good." Riley says walking into the kitchen.

"Thanks Riley. Now how about that appropriate greeting?" I say walking over to him and giving him a big hug.

"Watch it now Chloe, don't be getting all hands here, Char is looking right this way."

I smack the back of his head and finish pouring the wine.

"I'm ready to eat, it smells great Angel." Derricks says coming into the dining room.

"Good, well since we're all out here take a seat and I'll bring the food out to the table."

"I'll help." Char says following me into the kitchen.

Dinner turns out to be wonderful and everyone raves how good the food tastes. This is not only the first time I've used mom's recipes, it's the first time I've cooked for anyone like this at my apartment.

After we're all finished eating and the dishes are cleaned we decide to exchange some gifts in the living room. Char and Derrick head back to the bedrooms to grab their gifts while Riley and I grab drinks for the four of us.

The night continues with wrapping paper flying through the air, the guys acting like idiots with their new Red Sox gear and Char and I just sit back and enjoy the company. This is really nice and I love that they are here with me. I've made some great friends here in LA, but nothing beats being with family.

I glance over at the clock and see that it's almost midnight. Looking back toward the mounds of garbage I see that Derrick is watching me. Our eyes lock and he wiggles his eyebrows and shifts his head toward the bedroom. I blush and smile knowing exactly what it is he's referring to with his silent gestures.

"Well I don't know about you guys but I'm ready for bed. Is there anything you need before I shut down for the night?"

I stretch my arms above my head and show off a big yawn for emphasis. I don't know why I'm even trying to act sleepy. Both Riley and Char are looking at me knowing very well what is about to happen anyway.

"Nope, I'm not tired at all." Riley laughs.

"Stop Riley, let's give them some alone time. I think we're going to go for a ride and take a midnight stroll along the beach." Char says.

"Yeah sure okay, let me get you my keys so that you can let yourselves back in when you come back."

"Perfect thanks Chloe." Char says.

I walk on over to my purse and dig out my keys. Char is standing right behind me and I look up to see her smiling.

"Oh stop Char, it grosses me out knowing that you know what is about to happen."

"Seriously Chloe, I'm not a virgin. I know what sex is all about and if I lived on the opposite side of the country from Riley we'd have been naked by now."

"Okay great didn't need to know that or have the visual stuck in my head."

The two of us walk back into the living room. Riley and Derrick seem to be in an intense conversation.

"Are we interrupting a moment here boys?" Char asks with a giggle.

"Who us? Nope, I was just telling my boy right here the importance of safe sex and to text me when they are done. Come on babe, let's go make out in the car."

"What the hell Riley? Who the hell invited this guy?" I ask with a laugh. "Get out of my apartment you sex freak." I tell them leading both Char and Riley to the door.

I turn around still amused by what Riley just said and I catch site of Derrick watching me. His stare is intense and there's no expression on his face. He begins to walk over to me putting both hands on either side of my body against the door. My senses go into over load with the closeness to him. His breath is heavy on my neck and I can smell his cologne, the one that he very well knows makes me crazy.

"That was nice of them to leave us alone for a bit. I mean I'm not quite sure why they would have left you did say you were tired. I think I even saw a stretch and yawn a few minutes ago. You must be really exhausted. I think I should help you get into bed."

His eyes are fixed on mine and he's so close to me that if I moved just a little bit my lips would touch his.

"Well I do appreciate your generosity Derrick. I'm feeling kind of lazy. Would you mind helping me get out of this dress?"

"Of course, I would love to help you Chloe."

And then my world collides with Derrick. The bottom hem of my dress is now at my hips and he's lifting me so that my legs are around his waist. My arms are wrapped around his neck and his mouth is on mine. I have no clue how he's maneuvering, but somehow he's walking us to my room. I'm in a trance by his kiss but at the same time I have my eyes open in fear that my back is going to hit a wall. I trust Derrick with my life; however never before has he carried me while walking with his eyes closed in an apartment he just saw today.

Thankfully his skills are better than I gave him credit for and we're in my room. I've missed him so much and now we're alone. I want to be with Derrick, I need to be with Derrick.

DERRICK

Tonight has been great. Chloe's cooking skills amazed me yet again and she prepared a wonderful dinner for us. It really felt like Christmas day with my family. Even though everything was perfect there was just one other place I wanted to be…alone with Chloe in her room. All night I imagined being with her and now that dinner is over I need to bust a move and get to the presents part of the night. The quicker I can get this out of the way, the sooner I can get Chloe naked and in her bed.

The present portion of the night is taking a lot longer than I anticipated and fucking Riley is being a complete child. He continues to play with all my Red Sox gear from Chloe and if he doesn't knock it the hell off I'm going to punch him in the head. He knows I'm tied up over Chloe and the fact that I still have yet to touch her has me going nuts.

Then out of the blue I see Chloe looking toward the clock on her wall. I give her a suggestive look once her eyes meet mine and my girl is off and running. She mentions to Char and Riley that she is tired from the day and even throws out a stretch and yawn for good measure, that's my girl.

After an awkward moment, courtesy of Riley, he and Charlie are out the door to give us some alone time. Thank you Jesus.

Chloe and I are alone, fucking really alone. I stare at her as she closes the door and all I can think about is running my tongue all over her body. She has the sweetest taste in the world and the damn dress is hiding her gorgeous body that is calling my name. I walk closer to her and place a hand on either side of her head against the door. This is our moment and I'm taking in all of her for myself. With a little fun banter I chose to end this fiasco and get her into her bed. Picking her up I walk us back to the bedroom and kick the door shut with my foot. With my obvious ninja coordination I made it back here eyes closed with no injuries.

I lye her down on her bed and hover over her body. Spreading my legs on either side of her hips I use my arms to keep my weight off of her. I trail kisses from the tip of her nose to her chin down along the sides of her jaw and place little licks on both sides of her neck. She squirms under me and let's out slight moans to let me know what I'm doing to her is driving her mad. There's no way I plan to take tonight fast with her. It has been way to long that we have been together like this.

I lean back on my feet and pull her into a sitting position. Grabbing the hem of her dress I guide it along her body and over her head. She sits there completely naked, good god this woman is going to kill me.

"Not only are you absolutely beautiful Chloe, but you're driving me nuts. Had I known you were wearing nothing under this dress I never would have let you escape from me earlier."

Chloe lets out a giggle and climbs herself into my lap.

"Derrick I have missed you so much and I've been doing a lot of thinking about how hard it's for us to be apart so much."

I don't know where she is going with this, but if she feels half as shitty as I do about our long distance relationship I need to shut her up before we have this conversation.

"Love, let's not talk about this now. I want to be with you tonight, just us all night."

I kiss her hard and give her all the emotions that have bottling up over the past few weeks. It kills me that I only get her like this every few months. I have no idea how we will ever make this work, but for fucks sake, I'm not questioning it tonight. I need to be deep inside her pouring out my love to her like only we know how to do.

With her sitting in my lap I spread her legs so that she can straddle my thighs. She puts her arms around my neck and connects her lips to mine. Our kiss starts out slow this time and she moves in just close enough so that her bare breasts are up against my shirt covered chest. I want so badly to be skin to skin with her so I push her back. Starting to undo the buttons on my shirt, she bats my hands away.

"Let me, please." She says in such a seductive voice.

I nod in approval and watch her as she slowly undoes each button one at a time. Once she has finished she looks up at me through her thick lashes and gives me a killer smile. She pushes the shirt off of my shoulders and runs her hands down my arms. Her light touch is sending warmth through my body and I want to toss her onto this bed and bury myself into her. But I can't. I want to take this slow.

I smile back at her and allow her to seduce me. I don't care how long it takes. I'll patiently wait and just watch her as her hands work their magic along my body.

"Let's stand you up so that I can get these jeans off." She says.

I listen and do as she says. I feel like a soldier and she is my drill instructor. I know that I'll do anything she asks of me, it's how it has always been with us. She is my obsession and I'll follow her as she guides me where she wants me.

Standing in front of her she undoes the button to my jeans and pulls down the zipper. Her hands come back up to my chest and while she traces her fingers along my skin she peppers kisses from my collar bone to my chest down to the light trail of hair that leads into my boxer briefs.

"I've wanted to do this since you walked into my apartment."

She sticks her thumbs into my pants near my hips and pulls down my jeans and briefs. She follows them down to the floor and helps me step out one foot at a time. She runs her hands up my calves to my thighs and grabs my balls in her hands. By now my dick is standing at full attention and in a blink of an eye she has me in her mouth.

"Holy fuck Chloe!" I groan.

She giggles and continues on her mission to break my manhood. With a quick pace she sucks me into the back of her throat and then runs her hand up and down my length in a jerking motion. This feels so damn good I don't know how long I'll be able to hold out before I cum all over her mouth.

"Angel as good as you're making me feel you have to slow down. We haven't been together in a few weeks and I'm about to explode."

Chloe moves from her position and begins to stand in front of me.

"How about you get that sweet ass of yours in bed so I can make love to you?"

"Oh I like that idea, come on lover boy. Help me remember why I love you so much."

Chloe slides over onto her bed and moves herself up to the pillows. Her dark hair is now like a blanket along the top of her bed and I just stare at all of her beauty.

"You're so beautiful Chloe, this moment makes the past few weeks worth the wait."

"I'm glad you think so, now come here and kiss me Derrick."

"Your wish is my command Angel."

Chapter 14

CHLOE

"God this week is flying by." Char shouts as she throws her body onto the couch. "Please tell me you don't have any other activities planned for us while we're here."

I laugh at the dramatic show my sister is putting on even though I know she is having a good time.

"Come on Char, a lot of the things we've been doing were on your bucket list. So stop your bitching." I say as I toss a water bottle in her direction.

"Yeah, I know. I'm just not used to all this activity. I'm an accountant remember not an extreme sports professional."

"Well I beg to differ baby you sure as hell have the stamina of an extreme sports professional when we're alone and in the bedroom." Replies Riley.

"Oh my god, I really didn't need to hear that." I screech and run off into my bedroom.

As I strip myself out of my clothes from our rock climbing mission I hear the bedroom door shut. I can only assume it's Derrick and my heart picks up its pace. I know that I love him with all that I am, but something seems to be off between the two of us this visit. When we're together the physical chemistry is out of this world, but it's almost as if our emotional bond is starting to crack. Maybe it's the fact that we haven't seen one another for a few weeks, I'm not sure. But I do know that it scares me.

A light knocking sound vibrates the bathroom door.

"Can I come in love?" Derrick asks.

"Do you really need to ask Derrick? Come on in and get in the shower with me." I shout back while turning on the water.

Steam begins to fill the room and I close the shower curtain as the bathroom door shuts.

I can smell the scent of Derrick and my body starts to tingle. If this feeling is all I get right now I'm going to take it, I've missed him too much to miss any opportunity to be with him.

He slides the curtain just enough for him to enter the shower with me.

"Well hello there beautiful." He says with a big smile on his gorgeous face.

"Hello to you too handsome." I reply.

"I just wanted to be close to you again so I thought this would be the perfect opportunity. Let me wash you Chloe, let me love you." He says.

His lips slowly start to kiss me and warmth spreads throughout my body. He nibbles on my lower lip till I open my mouth for him. His tongue is warm and tastes like mint. I love the way he kisses me. I love the way he takes care of me like this. Derrick's hands run from my shoulders down to my hands bringing them up to his neck. He grabs my ass and lifts me up, my legs going around his waist. My back is pushed up against the shower wall and our kiss becomes a frenzy of nips, our tongues dancing, and quiet moans of pleasure. I can feel he's happy to be with me as his erection grows between our bodies.

"I want to be with you now Chloe, not later. I'm tired of waiting to be one with you. This is killing me Angel." He says looking into my eyes.

Seeing the pain he feels kills me. I wish there was a way for us to be closer, the distance is getting harder and harder every time we have to say see you later.

"Derrick I want you with me now. We're together now, I need you so bad." I tell him and then crash my mouth onto his.

"Oh god Chloe I love you so much."

"I love you too Derrick. Please don't make me wait another second."

Derrick takes that as his cue to move this a bit faster. He grabs his length and pushes it into my entrance. The initial response from my body is a hint of pain from his size but as he fully enters my body pleasure kicks into full gear.

"Shit Chloe you're so warm and tight. It feels to damn good to go slow, this is happening fast love so enjoy the ride."

"Oh I will." I respond with a smile.

Our bodies connect and give us an out of this world experience. Pumping himself in and out of my body brings me such pleasure, but nothing sends me over the edge like watching where our bodies meet. We both look down to the connection we're sharing and within seconds we're both falling to an unbelievable climax. We look into each other's eyes and something happens. I'm not quite sure, but in this moment I feel as if our souls just said goodbye.

I am so torn. My heart belongs to this man, why am I feeling like this?

We stay connected for a few moments, both of us realizing something just happened. The relationship we've always shared, the bond we swore would never break…just cracked and together we saw the splinter begin to spread.

Eventually, after who knows how long, we pull away from one another and wash our bodies in silence.

The next few days are relaxing while the four of us lay around lazy in the apartment. Char had just about enough activity to last her a few decades while Riley and Derrick agreed it would be nice to live as couch potatoes for the remainder of the trip. Between watching movies and ordering take out, I was getting anxious to go back to my regular routine.

The thought of going back to my daily life is exciting and scary all at the same time. I'm not too worried about the aftermath of Char and Riley going home, it's the fact that once again I would have to say goodbye to Derrick.

Saturday morning the four of us got up early to see Char and Riley off at the airport. I loved every moment of their visit and can see how much these two love each other. I'm so happy for Char that she has found her soul mate. She deserves it after everything she's been through.

"So when can we expect to see you in the Boston area?" Char asks before heading through security.

"God, I have no clue. The playoffs are starting soon, Super Bowl is coming up in a few weeks, and then March Madness starts. It's going to be a busy couple months for me."

"Okay well don't be a stranger Chloe, we love you." She says giving me a tight squeeze.

"I love you guys too. Take care of my baby sister Riley." I say with a punch to his arm.

"Will do Chloe. Give me a wink next time you're on the air." He says with a big grin.

I giggle at his comment and nod my head.

Derrick and I walk out to my car once again in silence. Ever since our moment in the shower the other day things have been different between us. I hate to mention anything and have it blow up in my face while he is here, but the anxiety is eating at me.

When we get back to my apartment I head into the guest room and try to busy myself cleaning up after Char and Riley. This is how I calm myself when I don't want to think about the present, I keep myself busy with chores.

I walk through the living room to get to the laundry and see Derrick sitting on the couch watching a movie.

"Are you going to clean today or come and talk to me about what's going on Chloe? I know you and can tell what you're doing." He says as I walk past him.

"I just want to get this stuff started so I don't have to worry about it later." I reply keeping on my mission to avoid a conversation I don't want to have.

Derrick follows me into the laundry room and takes the basket from my hands.

"Chloe we need to talk. We should have talked about this the other day. It can't wait any longer. I'm breaking the silence before it eats us both alive."

The look on his face is the same look I saw years ago before I left for college. But this time it feels like we're saying goodbye...not see you later.

DERRICK

The visit to LA has been both an adventure and lazy...if those two things are even possible together. Chloe has slammed so many sightseeing and extreme sporting activities into this week I think we all deserve to be lazy for the rest of the vacation.

After we get back from rock climbing Charlie and Riley pass out on the couches while I follow Chloe back to her bedroom to take a shower. She seems to be a bit off when we're alone together, but I know that if I can connect with her physically we'll both remember why we mean so much to one another. It's not just about the sex, which is always great, but about the actual way our bodies connect like a puzzle.

The past has been a challenge for us, but this distance is almost too much to bear. I need to be with her as much as possible and get my fill of Chloe when I can.

I knock on the bathroom door and ask, "Can I come in love?"

Chloe responds and I don't hesitate to open the door and strip myself of my clothes. I open the shower curtain and stare at Chloe as the water cascades down her body. Chloe is fortunate that she doesn't have to do much to keep up with her sexy physique. She has a tone belly, perky tits, and a set of legs that I wish were attached to my waist at all times.

Our kiss starts off slow while her and my body come against one another. Immediately I feel like I'm on fire from her touch. I nibble her lower lip waiting for her to open her lips and welcome my kiss a little deeper. I run my hands from the top of her shoulders down to her hands locking them behind my neck for support. I grab her sweet little ass and lift her up so that her legs are around my waist. I push her back up against the shower wall and kiss her like it's the last time we'll be like this together.

"I want to be with you now Chloe, not later. I'm tired of waiting to be one with you. This is killing me angel." I say looking into her eyes.

"Derrick I want you with me now. We're together now, I need you so bad." She tells me and then crashes her mouth onto mine.

We share our love for one another like only we know how. I grab onto my cock and push into her heat. Her body tenses to the sudden push, but once I'm fully inside of her she picks up a rhythm of her own.

She is warm and tight, I know I won't last long like this.

I pump myself in and out of her body bringing myself closer to my breaking point. The sounds of Chloe's moans encourage me to move faster. I look down at her and see she is watching my movements sliding in and out of her body. We both watch the connection we're sharing in this moment and with a loud groan I let myself fall to pieces inside of my angel. She looks up into my eyes and I see something I never thought I would experience with her…goodbye.

The silence and the lack of the connection we always shared. Something is happening and I'm scared to find out what's going on between us. Since the shower the other day we really haven't spoken more than a few words to each other. We haven't even touched each other more than holding hands or a kiss to the cheek.

We've just taken Charlie and Riley back to the airport and the first thing she does when we get back is start cleaning. I can't deal with this anymore, one of us has to start this conversation and at this point no matter what the outcome I've got to get these feelings off my chest.

She walks past me through the living room into the laundry. I get up off the couch and follow her, it's now or never. We need to talk.

I grab the wash basket from her hands and set it on the washing machine.

Lifting her hands to my lips I give them a kiss and tell her, "Chloe we need to talk. We should've done this the other day. I can't wait any longer. One of has to break the silence before it kills us both."

A tear falls from her eyes onto my hand. I take her into my arms and hold her.

"Derrick I can't live without you in my life. You're my soul mate; we have to make this work."

"Chloe I want nothing more than to be with you forever, but we can't do this anymore. It hurts too much to be away from you. I respect your choice to move here for your career and I'm so proud of you for how far you've come."

"But…." She says in response.

"It's not fair Chloe. We have two separate lives hundreds of miles apart from each other. I want to marry you. I want to start a family with you. How can we do that living on opposite sides of the country?"

"Derrick, I want those things too."

"No Chloe. You may think you want them, but not as much as I do. I'm sorry Angel, but I just can't be with you and still be apart from one another like this."

I can feel Chloe's body become limp against mine and I ease her back into the living room.

Holding hands we sit on the couch and stare into space. The only sound that can be heard is our breathing and the cries that come from both our hearts.

Sobbing she looks at me and asks. "What does this all mean Derrick? Where does this leave us?"

I look back over at her and into her big brown eyes as a tear falls down my cheek.

"Chloe you were my first true love. And I'll always love you. Maybe in time things will change and I hope that we will still be open to have each other in our lives. It's just not good for either one of us to keep trying to make this work the way things are now. I'm going to book an earlier flight out for tomorrow morning. There's no reason to prolong this week when we both know and feel things are not the same as they've been in the past. I love you Chloe and will forever."

I let go of her hand and walk back into the extra bedroom. Closing the door I slam my back up against it and slide down to the floor. Tears pour from my eyes and my heart breaks into a million pieces. I never thought this day would come. We've just broken the strongest bond anyone could ever have. I know this is the best for both of us, but I just don't know why it hurts so badly.

I pull out my phone and through tear blurred eyes I scroll to my flight app and book a plane back home to Boston.

Chloe insists she come to the airport with me. I know it's not the best idea, but selfishly I say it's okay. She walks me to security and I stop just before having to walk through the screening booth. I bring her in close to me and kiss her on top of her head. My hands run through her long dark hair and the smell of her mango shampoo sends thousands of memories through my mind. The last piece of my heart has just broke and tears pool in my eyes. I'm doing my best to hold myself together for her sake, but it really is pointless. My heart is now completely shattered and the love of my life is about to walk away from me for good.

I pull away from her and look into her eyes. She really is the most beautiful woman in the world and I'm so glad she was mine.

"Derrick, I love you so much."

"I love you too Chloe"

I let go of her hands and walk up to the security check. Turning around I see her still standing there with her arms wrapped around her waist.

She wipes away her tears and she mouths "goodbye love".

And then she turns and walks away.

Part Two
Moving On

Chapter 15

CHLOE

As I walk back to my car the tears begin to flood my vision. Time away from one another is something we have dealt with for years, but taking time to be apart is something I never thought we would have to deal with. The realization of what just happened in the airport is kicking in…no longer are Derrick and I a couple…it's over.

I just don't understand how this all happened, we were always so happy. No matter how far apart we were from one another we always found a way to make us work. Now I feel like we have just given up on something that was so special to both of us.

I don't know what I'm going to do.

While wiping away the tears I get into my car and pull out my phone. Hoping there would be some sort of message from Derrick, I sigh when my screen is blank. My whole life has been about me and Derrick and now I'm a hot fucking mess.

Without another thought I push send on the phone hoping the other line will pick up.

"I already heard." She says before I can even get a word out.

"But how, I mean why, did he call you the minute I walked away from him?" I ask sobbing into the phone.

"Chloe you have to understand his side here too. I love you both so much, but it wasn't easy for him when you chose NYU over Harvard or when you took the job in LA. I can't imagine what it's like to only see one another every other month or so. How long did you think this would go on before one of you decided to make a decision?"

"God damn it Char, can't you be on my side here for once? My heart is breaking and you're telling me you knew this would happen. Don't you think I know that my choices are what pushed him away? Here I thought we were going to spend a great week together and all it turned out to be was a romantic goodbye."

I can barely breathe let alone speak. It's so hard to believe that today was the last time I would hold him, kiss him and tell him I love him.

"He's the love of my life Char, how am I supposed to be okay with all of this?"

"I don't know Chloe. All I can say is give it time, just like you told me a few months ago. If you two are meant to be you will find your way back together."

"As insightful as you sound right now it doesn't make me feel any better."

"I know, keep yourself busy and focus on the reason you moved to LA."

"Yeah, okay. Thanks Char, I'll call you later this week."

The line goes dead, no I love you Chloe…be strong Chloe…nothing. She is totally on his side through this and that is exactly how it should be. I'm the one that did this to us. It was my decision to choose a career over the love of my life. Now I just have to deal with it and pretend like I am not nursing a broken heart.

The next few weeks fly by and I feel like I'm living in a daze. I put on my best face when I'm at work and in front of the camera, but it takes just about all I have through the day not to break down and call Derrick. I've kept in constant touch with Char and can't believe she answers the phone when I call. She's been helping me get through this, but I worry that my emotional state will make her refuse my contact soon. All I really know right now is that Derrick has drowned himself in some pretty big cases at work and goes out with Riley when he can. I'm happy he's still living but it kills me that he's surviving without me.

I need to pull my shit together somehow and either focus on my career or pack it all back up and move home. But I know I can't do the latter choice, I've come too far in my career to give it all up.

The thing that sucks is that I finally landed the job of a lifetime, this is all I've ever wanted to do and staying here doing what I love cost me the one person in the world that matters more to me than anything.

The next few weeks at work are a big deal for me professionally. The freaking Super Bowl is coming up and I've been interviewing a rookie quarterback that will probably take his team all the way. I can't screw this up, I have to get my head back on track, build a schedule and give ESPN all that I can.

I'm pulled out of my trance by a knock on my door. I look up and see my co-host Trent. With a professional smile I take in a deep breath and stand to walk his way.

"You okay Chloe? We're on in a few minutes and I thought I should come and look for you. It's not like you to be in the office ten minutes before we are live."

"Yep I'm coming, umm, just wanted to check on some things before it was time. Guess I was in here longer than I expected. Thanks for coming to check on me." I tell him refusing to make eye contact.

Trent has been one of the crew members that always seemed to be there when I started to get homesick. He too is far away from home and chose career over love so of course he knows what I'm going through. Wait no correction, what I was going through. I haven't had it in me to share the news with my friends. I really don't want to talk about it with anyone.

He puts his hand on the small of my back and guides me out the door and over to where our shoot takes place every day in the EPSN studio.

"You know a bunch of us are going out after work tonight if you want to come. I think it would be good for you to get out. You haven't been the same since Derrick went back home." He says taking his seat on the stage.

"We'll see. I'm not really up for going out tonight."

"Chloe Taylor, get your head out of your ass and come on out with us tonight." A voice sounds from behind the green screen.

"When you put it like that Andrew, how can I refuse?" I tell him with a smile.

Andrew Lock is a rookie quarterback for the Allentown Colts and will be on our show again tonight. He's been the prime time athlete on majority of shows for the past few months because of his strong ability to take his team to the Super Bowl in a few weeks.

"It's not every week I'm in town and can spend a night out with my favorite sport's analyst." He says with a wink.

"Cool it Lock, you know Chloe is well spoken for back home. Lay off the pretty boy smirks." Trent says moving to stand.

"Whoa boys settle down. Chloe isn't going home with anyone tonight. It's just drinks, relax Tarzan." I say in Trent's direction giving him the evil eye.

"Well word on the street says that Chloe isn't spoken for anymore so I say we see how tonight goes and take it from there." Andrew says looking right at me, my mouth gapped wide open.

"Chloe what the hell is going on and what does Lock know that I don't?" Trent says sitting back down.

"Ugh never mind Trent, we are on in like 30 seconds." I tell him while organizing my notes in front of me and placing my glass of water directly to my left.

DERRICK

Watching her walk away from security was like ripping out my heart.

This past week was painful in more ways than one and the feeling I had told me it was time to leave. After Charlie and Riley left on Saturday I thought for sure Chloe and I would be on cloud nine. We planned on spending a lot of time in the apartment so that no moment would be lost. The problem was that when we were alone something felt like it was missing or that we were forcing one another to do things that used to come so naturally to us. It got to the point that I couldn't bare it any longer and I had to break the silence.

I told the only woman that I've ever loved that the distance from her was too hard to bear. Every spare moment I had I was obsessing about her and what she was doing. I hated that she had a life so far away from mine and I too was creating a life without her in it. It wasn't like I wanted to see other people. She's the only one I could ever love. I just can't consume myself with a future we both know is not going to happen.

After our talk at her place we both decided it was best to take some time apart.

So I decided to book and earlier flight and leave Sunday morning…four whole days before I was supposed to head home to Boston.

Now I sit here waiting to board a plane and all I can do is pray I don't regret the decision we just made.

I pull out my cell and am so tempted to send her a text to tell her how sorry I am and that it will be okay. But I can't…because it won't.

Instead I call Charlie and let her know what just happened.

"Hey Derrick, what's up? You guys bored without us already?" Charlie says.

"Umm not really, I'm actually at the airport waiting to catch a flight." I reply.

"What?" She screams in the phone.

I can hear her telling Riley that I'm on my way home. And in the background he's asking her why.

"Look Derrick, whatever happened it will all be okay. When do you fly in? We'll come get you." She says in between telling Riley to shut up so she can hear me.

For a second a smile creeps on my face. Those two are nuts.

"I don't think it will be okay Charlie, but thanks anyway. I'll tell you about it when I get there. Pick me up around six. Oh, and Charlie, thanks."

I hit end on my phone and then shut it down. I need to distance myself from everyone.

Boarding the plane was simple. It was realizing why I was on the plane that killed me inside.

For eight years Chloe Taylor was my world. She was the reason I wanted to be a good man, have a great job, and find a way in life that would support both of us as we built a family. Now all those dreams are gone. I know in my mind we made the right decision, but I can't convince my heart and now its breaking.

A tear begins to roll down the side of my face as I punch the pillow and lay my head up against the cabin wall.

I close my eyes and try to get some sleep. Once I get back to Boston I have a lot of things I need to do.

The last few weeks have flown by and I'm swamped with three case loads that leave me no time to even think. Thankfully tonight I'm going to head over to Riley and Charlie's for dinner and then out to the pub with Riley and some of the guys. I deserve some time to enjoy myself instead of having my head stuck in the office.

I walk down the street to their house. It still kind of cracks me up that these two bought a house down the block from me. Between the two of them they've done everything they can to keep me in line and on track with the things that are important like food, sleep, and clean underwear.

When I reach their front porch Riley and his dog Manny are waiting for me outside. Manny runs down to the sidewalk to greet me and Riley has a big smile on his face.

"What the hell has you so happy today?" I ask him.

"Well besides the fact I have the best girlfriend in the world, I taught Manny a new trick today."

"Oh yeah, dare I ask what this trick may be?" I reply giving him a glare.

Only Riley can spend hours with his dog and teach him to do the stupidest things. Just last week he tried to get him to flush the toilet after he took a shit. Riley was so excited he called me and Charlie in the bathroom to watch. Too bad for us we didn't realize what was in the toilet until it was too late.

"Look man, I promise there's no shit involved this time. Come on, you'll love it."

"Okay Manny let me see what you got." I tell him.

"Manny, come here boy. Listen boy, its Miller time go get it boy." Riley yells while opening the front door.

What the hell is he up to and what does Miller time mean to a dog.

Just then Manny comes running out to me on the porch with a bottle of Miller in his mouth.

"No shit, man's best friend is now man's best bartender. Way to go Manny. You two should go on the road with this stuff."

"Very funny Derrick, don't encourage him. Next thing I know Manny will be vacuuming the rugs for us." Charlie says while coming over to me and giving me a tight squeeze.

"And how would that be a bad thing, less cleaning for you babe." Riley says grabbing her from me and kissing her on the forehead.

"Come on in you fools and eat some food before you head out to the pub."

We follow Charlie inside and take a seat at the table. I'm so grateful for these two people in my life. As crazy as they are, they are pretty much all I got right now.

"Oh hey Derrick, I forget to tell you my sister Emma is coming up for a visit next weekend. She may need a place to crash for a few weeks. Can she take my old room at your house?" Riley asks and piles a fork full of food in his mouth.

"Wait, what? Why can't she stay here?" I ask looking at the two of them.

Charlie places her hand on Riley's and responds for him. "Well it's kind of complicated and Riley doesn't want Emma's husband to know that she is staying up here in Boston. So just in case he comes up here we don't want her in the house."

"Well then of course she can. It's not like I'm ever home and I have the extra space."

"Great, thanks man. I'll let her know."

I guess it will be nice to have a roommate again…we will see.

Chapter 16

CHLOE

After some convincing on Trent's part and Andrew twisting my arm, I agree to go out with the crew for a drink after our session has wrapped up. I agree that I've been a hermit the past few weeks, but I have a valid reason. The love of my life is now living his life without me.

I walk back to our office to grab my things when a warm arm swings across my shoulders pulling me into a hug.

"Come on Chloe, you can drive with me. I think we have a lot to talk about anyway." Trent says with a raised eyebrow.

"Trent, don't give me that look." I respond.

"Chloe you're one of my closest friends here in LA. I tell you about my crazy shit everyday at lunch. You can't keep the fact that you and Derrick broke up a secret."

The look on his face is that of hurt. He's right; he has been a good friend to me since we both moved out here.

"Alright, I understand how this could be a bit upsetting for me to have omitted this tiny detail. But to be honest Trent, I really didn't want to talk to anyone about it."

"I get it Chloe. I really do, but you shouldn't hold in this kind of stuff. After all, your family and friends are on the other side of the country and you don't have anyone here to really turn to for support. Just know that you will always have me as a friend to be there; especially while that douche Lock is all up in your game."

I laugh off his comment as we walk together to our office. I grab my purse and keys and we're out the door.

Trent escorts me out of the building and being the gentleman that he is opens the car door for me.

The ride over to the club is quiet and I appreciate the time to think to myself. Telling Trent about Derrick and I is something I really need to do and it may even help to get some of the stress off of my chest. Maybe I'll invite him to lunch over the weekend and we can chat. Yeah, that sounds good.

"So are you ready for…lights, camera and action when we get here?"

"Umm, I don't know what you mean. Why would there be cameras? We always come here and no one ever makes a big deal about it."

"You're right we always do come here, but you do realize who else is coming here tonight?" He asks giving me a look of amusement.

"Oh." I reply. It's really all I can muster.

Andrew is coming out with us tonight. I hadn't thought about the publicity that will bring with us to our favorite spot. Oh well, we'll just have to deal with it I guess. I'm still unsure of Andrews's motive when it comes to him perusing me. He can have just about any girl out there. Why is he constantly harassing me? I shake off my thoughts for a moment as I see the lights of the club ahead.

Trent pulls up to the front of the club. As the valet guy comes over to the car Trent gets out and comes around to open my door for me. There doesn't seem to be a big commotion outside so he leads me to the entrance and we make our way back to a large section in the back filled with soft leather booths and tables. Since we're expecting a larger group tonight, this will be perfect.

A few minutes later the rest of the ESPN Live crew come into the club and Trent waves them back our way. Some of the other analysts crowd into our section along with a few of the camera and makeup crew members.

Looking around at all the people that surround me, I never really felt close with that many people here in LA besides Trent. I seem to have put up a guard not allowing many people into my close circle. My real friends and family are all back in Boston, but I chose to move away and follow my dreams.

I don't know if I'm supposed to stretch my wings and start anew now that Derrick and I are no longer a couple. It has been a little over a month since he left…and not a word, text or anything.

I smile as I gaze around this group. This is my family, these are my friends and I believe it's time to bring down some walls. Indeed it's time to move on and make new friends, after all LA is my home and nothing is going to change that. Not only do I have these fine people, I also have my Cousin Lucy's best friend Sam out here. I really need to give her a call. A full girl's day may be exactly what I need right about now. I haven't spent a day at the spa since Char was out here for New Year's. I'm well overdue.

I stand and move toward Trent. He's talking to another analyst and I don't want to interrupt their conversation. Instead I put my hand on his shoulder and signal with a nod that I'm heading to the bar.

Being here tonight I have a sense of freedom. I'm not sure if it's the decision to break down my walls or just being in this environment. I feel happy and that is something I haven't felt in a few weeks.

I spot an opening up at the bar and slide my way in between a tall guy and a group of ladies. The female bartender flies past me and I breathe out a sigh of annoyance. I feel a warm hand press against my back and hear a whistling sound behind my right ear. The guy next to me rolls his eyes as the female bartender saunters over to the guy invading my space from behind.

"What can I get you tonight handsome?" She asks.

Oh god, I roll my eyes right back at her direct flirting.

"I'll have two Miller Lite bottles and whatever this beautiful lady wants." He says moving in closer to my body so that I can feel his legs against the back of mine.

"I'll have a glass of Moscato, please." I tell the bartender.

I turn my head to look at this mystery man and once I gaze over my shoulder I see who is pressing his body against me.

Of course the bartender was right, he is indeed very handsome. With his bright green eyes, dark brown hair and hypnotizing smile, it's none other than Andrew Lock.

Since he has me pinned against the bar and both of his arms are now on either side of me, I attempt to turn my body to face his.

"Well hello there Andrew." I say looking up through my thick, dark lashes.

"Glad to see you came out to join me tonight." He replies.

I giggle at his forwardness.

"Oh Andrew, you seem to have a misconception of me. I didn't come out here to be with you. Why don't you take a look toward the back of the club?" I say in a soft seductive tone.

He turns his head to look and I glance at his defined jaw and a hint of stubble that has grown in since I saw him earlier today.

"Yes, those are the people I came here to be with tonight."

He bends his head down and I can feel his lips touch my hair.

"We'll see who can make you come the fastest." He says grazing his lips deeper into my hair skimming along my ear.

My body begins to tingle and I feel flushed by his comment. I need to get myself out of this situation with him. This is not something I'm ready for now or anytime soon for that matter.

I turn toward the bar and grab my glass of wine.

Bringing my body back to face Andrew, I thank him for the drink, give him a smile and lift his arm to make my way back to my friends.

DERRICK

I woke up this morning a bit earlier than I usually do, but I want to make sure things are in order for Emma, my new roommate. Charlie has gone out and bought a few things to help make the extra room a little more presentable. Well at least that what she said. Even though I think she wanted to make it look more girly. I still don't understand what was wrong with what I had in there. Riley never complained about the décor in the room.

Damn woman even did up the bathroom to match the bedding she purchased for the bedroom. I mean come on, whose house is this anyway….blah, I'm such a sucker.

Emma is coming into town today and will be moving her things into Riley's old room in my house. At first I thought it was a bit weird having a girl I didn't know move into Chloe and my house, but she is the older sister of one of my best friends. With everything Charlie and Riley have done for me the past few months, this is the least I can do to repay them. Besides, I have no clue if Emma will be here for a week or a year and I sure as hell am not using the space.

Charlie gave me a list of some things Emma likes and with all that she has been through I want her to feel at home here. I have a jam packed freezer and fridge full of foods and drinks we'll both be able to use and I even went out a bought a few other things so she'll feel welcome when she gets here this afternoon since I'll still be at work.

Lately I haven't been at home much, but still I want to make sure that Emma feels as though this is like a home for her. I can't imagine what she is going through, but any family of Riley's is immediately family of mine.

Charlie and I talked about this whole move and roommate situation for a while this weekend. As much as it will be nice to have someone else in the house, I still feel like Chloe should know. Charlie confirmed that she would let her know when the time was right. Since she is the one talking with her sister I said I was fine with that and left it alone. The next people I had to address were my parents.

The last thing I needed was for mom and dad to assume I had a girlfriend move in with me so soon after Chloe and I broke up. My poor mom, bless her heart, still thinks we're together and just on a little break. She swears that Chloe and I just need to find what is important to us and in time we will realize our love is strong enough to pull us back together. Hearing her say this shit is really starting to piss me off. Thank god Charlie was with me during mom's last rant. I think she finally sees my side of things and is willing to let it rest for right now.

I finally leave the house around 7:30 and make my way into the firm. I have a lot going on with three big cases. Work is all I've had to keep my mind off of Chloe and if I bring in these three cases as wins, I hope that the senior partners will consider giving me a promotion. I've done my fair share of work if I don't say so myself.

Getting right to work, I pull out a box of documents for a case I'll be working Friday morning. I get sucked into my work and before I know it the clock on the wall reads 1:30 ….fuck I was distracted.

My office phone rings for the tenth time in the past five minutes. I keep ignoring the call knowing it's one of the other junior partners Trisha. I know I told her we would head out for lunch today, but I really need to get this shit done for Friday's hearing.

I've been working day and night on this case and there's no way in hell I'm going to lose this fight. A multi-billion dollar pharmaceutical company is going through a law suit and our firm, Jax and Paige, are defending the consumers. With the amount of detail I have found from the manufacturer, the shipping plant and the victims this one should be a no brainer. It just sucks that I'm going up against a fellow alumni of Harvard.

A sound of knocking pulls my eyes from my desk to the door where Trisha now stands.

"Derrick come on, you have to eat. Those documents will all be sitting right there when you come back in an hour." She says walking this way.

I watch her as she comes closer to my desk. Trisha is an attractive woman. She's tall and you can definitely tell that she takes good care of her body. Her hair is a light blonde with darker blonde highlights and she has big blue eyes. Her features are very feminine and the closer she gets to me the more I can smell her sweet perfume.

Ordinarily I wouldn't be checking her out like this, but I'm overly stressed and in dire need of some female attention.

As that thought passes through my mind I instantly think of Chloe. The way we left one another was heartbreaking and I haven't heard from her since. Charlie keeps me up to date on her well being, but since last weekend I stopped asking. There really is no use torturing myself anymore. Even Charlie and Riley said I need to get out more and have fun. Maybe going to lunch with Trisha counts as going out? I'm sure we could have fun.

I slip myself out of my train of thought and back to the woman standing in front of me.

"I'm sorry Trisha, what were you saying?" I ask raking up the papers across my desk.

"Geez Derrick, I thought you were lost in thought there for a moment." She says sitting down at the chair across from me and my desk.

"Sorry, I spaced out for a minute."

"It's okay. So you want to join me for lunch?" She asks crossing her left leg over her right.

Damn it Derrick, pull your shit together. It's been awhile since I've been with a woman, but shit there's no need to be sporting a boner right now. I move in my chair and attempt to adjust myself under the desk.

"Yeah, lunch sounds good. Give me ten minutes and I'll meet you out front."

"Great, don't be late. I'm starving." She says getting up from the chair and walking out my office door.

I watch as her ass sways and her long legs take her out of my sight.

Hmm, starving…she doesn't know the half of it.

Chapter 17
February 2013

CHLOE

Sitting in my office I lean back into my black leather chair and shut my eyes. I'm exhausted from last night. The Allentown Colts won the Super Bowl and Andrew Lock made good on his promise of taking his team all the way undefeated. It was the most amazing experience working on the field with the coaches and players. I felt at home being next to the live action.

Thankfully today was an easy wrap up day and final interviews with some of the players. I feel wiped out and ready to relax with some good friends that I haven't seen in a while. My cousin Lucy that I went to NYU with and her boyfriend Chase have come to LA for a visit. Trent and I have plans to meet up with them and Lucy's best friend Sam along with Sam's…..I'm not exactly sure what he is to her, but his name is Jax.

I giggle at the drama that has consumed those three and then I'm brought back to reality.

My bosses Tom, Traci and ugh douche bag, king of sexual harassment Mark walk into the office.

The two men continue to stand and Traci takes a seat in one of the chairs across from my desk.

"Congrats Taylor! How does it feel to cover the winning team for the Super Bowl?" Tom asks.

"It feels amazing, but to be honest, I'm so glad it's done and over. I had myself so worked up about it. I guess I was nervous about the crowd, the fans and the team. It's a lot to take in at one time, but I loved every moment of it."

"You're a natural Chloe. You need to get out behind that desk and out on the field with the teams. It suits you much better." Traci says with a smile.

"Thanks Traci that is a huge compliment. Maybe a spot will open up one day and if it's meant to be…I'll go for it."

Just saying that phrase sends chills through my body. I can hear Char's voice in my head saying those exact words the day Derrick left LA. *If you two are meant to be you will find your way back together.* A lump forms in my throat and I can feel my hands go numb from the grasp I have them in. Ugh, will this pain ever go away.

"Hey Chloe, you okay? You spaced out on us there for a second." Traci says waving her hand in front of my face.

"Oh yeah, sorry. I was thinking about what you just said. It would be amazing to be on the field as an analyst."

"Well I've heard a few things from the other ESPN offices. There's a position opening up with a team. You'd have a solid home spot, no traveling, but it isn't in LA." Mark says giving me a look with his eyebrows scrunched.

Ugh, I would do just about anything to get away from that slime ball and his roaming hands. I don't care who his daddy is, he shouldn't treat women like we're a piece of meat.

Before we can finish our conversation Trent walks over. Thank goodness my savior arrives.

"You ready to go superstar?"

I laugh at his comment and give him the evil eye.

"You guys want to come with us? We're going to get some dinner and a few drinks. After the Super Bowl yesterday I need a night to unwind."

"Nah, I'm good you guys go ahead." Traci says.

"Chloe we'll pick up this conversation later. It may be something you want to look into." Mark says.

Tom just nods his head and walks out the door.

"Thanks Tom, see you tomorrow." I shout.

Trent and I wave as we walk down the hallway and into the elevator.

"What was that all about?" Trent asks.

"Nothing really, just another position that they think could suit me better."

"You're not leaving me are you?" He asks with a pout.

"Stop it loser. I'm not making any plans till I hear them out. Besides I don't want to think about work tonight. Let's have fun. Lucy, Sam and Jax should be meeting us at the club in an hour."

"Perfect cause I'm starving."

I laugh at him and walk out of the elevator and toward my car.

Trent and I drop off his car first and then head over to my apartment to leave mine for the night as well. There's no use taking both cars and having to leave one behind if we're too drunk to drive.

The cab pulls up and Trent and I dash out of the lobby and into the waiting car before someone else snags it away.

Within only fifteen minutes we're at the club and waiting inside for the rest of our friends.

I take a seat in one of the larger booths along the wall and Trent goes up to the bar to get us each a drink. While waiting I spot Lucy and Sam walking into the club. I get out of the booth and stand tall waving my arms. Finally they see me and wave back. Once they are both in front of me we embrace one another in a giant hug and will burst into a fit of giggles. It's so good to be back with these two ladies, they are so much fun to be with.

Shortly after our group hug we pile into the booth as Chase, Trent and Jax come over with our drinks.

"Well thanks gentlemen, how kind of you." Sam says winking at Trent.

I can see him blush, but at the same time his eye brows scrunch and I can tell exactly what he's thinking. I look him in the eyes and telepathically tell him, Sam is way out of your league. I don't want to be a bitch, but there is little nothing in common between these two and from the looks of it she may have her eyes on someone else.

"Come on ladies let's go out and show those girls on the dance floor how it's really done." Lucy shouts over the music.

"Damn biatch you're feisty tonight." Sam yells back with a smile.

"I'm game ladies, let's do this." I shout back and push Trent out of the booth so I can get out and hit the floor with my moves.

It's been way to damn long since I've had this much fun, let alone went out dancing with my girls.

The three of us find a spot on the floor and start to sway our hips just as Robin Thicke's song Blurred Lines begins to play across the club. We're having such a good time that I'm caught off guard when a strong arm grabs my waist and pulls me close.

I look into Lucy's eyes and she just smiles and shrugs her shoulders. Chase comes up behind Lucy and begins to grind into her. My eyes find Sam, but she is no help since she now has her arms wrapped around Jax's neck and they are swaying to a rhythm that is only theirs.

Unsure of whom this mystery man is behind me, I shimmy to the beat of the music and turn my body to face his. Not that I'm surprised at all, but the man now standing in front of me is Andrew Lock.

He looks down into my eyes and a huge smile crosses his face. His eyes sparkle in the lights of the club and he pulls me closer to his body.

"You just can't take a hint can you Lock?" I ask pulling my arms up and around his neck.

"Nope and I have no plans on giving up on us Chloe. I believe its time you gave this a chance." He says bringing his face closer to mine so that his lips are once again in my hair.

"Well, I don't know what you're referring to as this, but a simple dance can't hurt for tonight." I say afraid of what his comeback may be.

"Oh Chloe you have no idea how badly I want to hurt you…it would feel so good." He says skimming the lobe of my ear with this hot breath.

My knees feel week with the words he says to me, but at the same time I have to be strong. This is one wall I'm not yet willing to let break down.

DERRICK

"Hey Derrick. Are you going to be home for dinner tonight?" Emma asks as we finish up our breakfast of fruit, yogurt and coffee.

We've found a pretty nice partnership between the two of us. Emma has only been living here for the past few weeks, but it's nice to know there is someone else here when I get home. Lately my schedule doesn't permit me to be home for dinner most nights however we both always make sure to have breakfast together each morning.

Emma is also a strong runner, so Riley and I head out with her every morning before we get ready for work. It's a good way to start the day and has quickly become a regular event and again I'm glad to have someone to do these things with.

"Nah, I won't be back till late tonight. Trisha and I are working on two new cases with each other this week and I figure we could just get take out and eat at the firm."

"That's silly Derrick, why don't you invite her over here after you're done at the office and you can eat some good home cooked food. I'm sure Trisha would rather eat my cooking than greasy take out."

"Sounds perfect, thanks Emma. I'll see you around seven, is that okay?"

"Yep, see you then. Have a good day Derrick." She says heading up the stairs.

I swallow down the last sip of my coffee, place the mug in the dishwasher and grab my briefcase before heading out the door.

For some reason I'm anxious to get to work today, actually to be honest I've been looking forward to going into work the past few weeks. The senior partners have brought Trisha and I together to work on the past few cases and I enjoy having someone with the same intellect to conduct some work.

Trisha is kind, funny and seems to know the right things to say at the right time. We're in sync with one another at the firm and I'm anxious to see how strong our chemistry is outside of the office working on our cases.

I stop at the local Dunkin Donuts before going to the office and pick us both up a coffee. I seem to work better when I'm extra alert on caffeine and the office stuff just doesn't seem to do the trick.

As soon as I pull into the parking garage, I park in my regular spot and walk over to the elevator. Juggling both cups of coffee I'm able to hit the #4 on the keypad, but not before a hand shoots through the doors.

I quickly push the <open door> button and in walks Trisha.

"Hey Derrick, thanks for holding the car for me." She says grabbing a cup of coffee out of my hand. "I assume this is for me?" She asks with a cute smile.

"A little presumptuous, aren't you?"

"Not really, it says my name on the side of the cup."

We both start to laugh as the elevator takes us up to the fourth floor and we exit the car. Both Trisha and I make our way over to my office and I start to lay out all the documents I had worked on the night before.

"Damn, Derrick it looks like you were burning the midnight oil on this last night."

"Pretty much, I kind of get drowned in my cases when I start them. It's just something I've always done. I don't want to miss anything that could be of use to the case."

"Smart man." Trisha says sitting down across from me at my desk.

"Indeed, I didn't get to where I am now with just my handsome face." I tell her taking a long sip of my coffee.

"Oh I'm sure." She replies with a wink.

I don't know if it's just me, but you could cut the sexual tension in this room with a knife.

"Yeah, that's how I roll. Hey I wanted to ask you, since we'll be working on this late again tonight, I was wondering if you want to come over to my place and work through dinner. My roommate Emma insists that I come home and eat rather than camping out here with greasy take out."

"Your roommate is female?"

That's all she got out of what I just said to her, ugh. The expression on her face is difficult to read. I can't tell if she is upset by this or surprised that I live with a girl.

In a nervous gesture, I run my fingers through my hair and look back at her.

"Yeah, I do. It's a long story, but she is the sister of one of my best friends Riley. She is having some marital issues and he asked that she stay with me for awhile. I've got the extra room, so I figured why not."

Her features begin to change and her prior expression changes into a smile.

"That is awfully sweet of you Derrick." She says placing her hand on mine and giving it a gentle squeeze.

I smile back at her and take my hand to pull out a few more things from my desk.

"Well now that all that is settled, let's get to work so there's less to do later tonight."

She repositions herself on the chair and clears her throat.

"Sounds like a plan to me." She says with a wink.

Trisha and I work side by side through the rest of day not even breaking for lunch. This is another huge case that involves a local school district and the busing company. Sometimes it amazes me the lengths people will do to save a buck. In my opinion, no dollar saved is worth the life of a student…or someone's child.

By the time six o'clock rolls around our stomachs are louder than our voices chatting amongst one another. A few times we look up and each other and laugh it off, but as of right now I think it's time to close up here and take the rest home.

"Are you about ready to get some dinner?" I ask.

"Hell yes, I'm starving. I thought you'd never stop working here." Trisha replies.

"Once you get me going it's hard to make me stop." I say with a smile.

I hear her mumble something under her breath, but it's hard to make it out…I think she just said, *wouldn't I like to know*. Damn is this girl flirting with me now? This should make for an interesting night at my place and even more awkward at work tomorrow. I can't let that happen. I have worked too hard to get where I am in this firm to mess it up now. We need to keep our relationship strictly professional…no matter what.

The two of us pack up the case documents and make our way out of the office and into the parking garage. Trisha says that she'll follow close behind me and promises to keep up knowing very well that I'm a speed demon and a starving one at that.

We reach my house in less than twenty minutes and Emma just about has dinner ready to go. I introduce the two ladies and they begin to chat about some of the upcoming events going on in Boston the next few weekends. While they are getting to know one another I run back out to my car and grab the two boxes of shit we'll need to work with. Once back inside I set the stuff down in the living room and make my way upstairs to change into something more comfortable.

When I come back down both ladies have a glass of wine in hand and a bottle of beer is waiting for me on the kitchen counter.

"Dinner should be ready in five minutes." Emma says.

"Sweet, thanks." I respond.

"So Emma here just told me about the story of her brother and your best friend meeting. How crazy was that?"

I laugh out loud remembering the first time they officially met in this very kitchen...*Charlie was the mini-mart bitch and Riley was the loon.*

"Yeah they're something else, but I can't imagine anyone else with Charlie. Riley is perfect for her and he makes her happy. That's all that really matters." I tell her.

Emma walks over to the stove, stirs up something in a pot and grabs down three bowls from the cabinet.

"I made chicken chili for dinner, I hope you like things hot."

I look over to Trisha and she smiles as her cheeks turn a deep shade of red. How cute, she's blushing.

The rest of the night goes off with no further sexual comments and Emma and Trisha seems to be getting along well. So well before I know it the clock reads eleven o'clock and we didn't even open the box of documents I drug home.

Oh well at least it was a nice relaxing night in the house. Lucky for me I had the company of two beautiful women, sucks that neither of them is the one that still holds my heart.

Chapter 18
April 2013

CHLOE

I flop down onto my soft black leather couch and let out a huge sigh. The past few weeks have been so tiring and I have to travel out of town in a couple days. I kick off my heels and lift my legs onto the couch.

Ever since I did the Super Bowl, I've been working directly with the players and coaches at the games as opposed to in the studio with ESPN Live. I know that Trent is missing me and totally hates his new partner, but I still meet up with him every chance I get.

Right now we're in the midst of college basketball with March Madness and getting closer and closer to the Final Four. This is the first time in my career that I've been able to attend a college basketball game. I had no idea how intense these guys are about their sport this time of year.

I've learned a lot in the past few months and excited about a new opportunity that is presenting itself to me. Luckily I've been a part of a major football event, basketball event and soon to be dabbling in a bit of my favorite sport, baseball.

After the conversation with my bosses, Tom, Traci and Mark, I took them up on the offer to look into a potential full time position working for a team as a permanent analyst. I like the idea of being in the middle of the action, watching the players doing what they do best and to be honest I would love to be closer to home. I haven't spoken a word to my parents or Char about this possible job offer yet. Having them know I could be working for the Red Sox and moving back home is just not something I'm ready to discuss.

I'm anxious for the job, it's something I would love to do, but at the same time I'm scared to death to live close to Derrick again. We haven't spoken a word to one another since he left, yet I still think about him every day.

I've been seeing more of Andrew the last few weeks, but nothing to concern myself with. I know he wants more, in more ways than one, but my heart still belongs to Derrick. I don't know why…I wish I could change how I feel…I just feel like he'll always be the one and I let him get away.

Andrew has been so patient with me and little by little I know I'm letting down my wall. I just do my best to keep my distance from his roaming hands and his lips away from my ears. There have been moments where I wanted to strip him of his clothes and lick every inch of him. Especially when he looks at me with those bright green eyes and smiles; however I have the willpower of a mule and refuse to give in to my sexual need.

He loves the idea that I may be moving back to the east coast. In fact he thinks it's a sign that we're meant to be together. I just laugh at his crazy thoughts and continue to tell him I'm not looking to get into any type of relationship…emotionally or sexually.

My phone starts to ring and I pry my sleepy ass from the couch and head out to the kitchen. I see it's Char and quickly hit the green accept button.

"Hi Char!" I sing with excitement.

I really do miss her, it's been a few months since we've been together and I need some time with her.

"Hey Chloe, how are you?" She asks.

"I'm doing pretty good. How are you and Riley?" I ask.

"Actually that is why I'm calling." She says.

"Why? What's wrong? Are you two okay?" I start to ramble off in question mode worried that something has happened.

"No silly, Riley and I are great. I just wanted to let you know some stuff that is going on here and it involves Riley's sister Emma and Derrick.

My heart starts beating out of my chest and I have to sit down. Emma and Derrick, what could she possibly mean?

"Chloe, you still there?" She asks.

"Umm, yeah I'm here. What's going on with them? Are they dating?"

Char starts to laugh on the other line. It gets to the point she is now laughing so hard that she puts the phone down and I hear it hit the table. What the fuck is going on?

"Chloe, hey it's Riley. What the hell did you do to make her laugh like that? I think she ran off to the bathroom before she pissed herself. Damn it woman."

"I have no clue. All I know is she wanted to tell me about Emma and Derrick. What's going on Riley?" I ask getting more pissed off the longer I wait for someone to answer me.

I know I have no right to get angry if Derrick is seeing someone else, but shit it hurts like hell.

"Oh, is that it? Why the hell is she laughing like a fucking hyena?" He asks with a chuckle.

"I don't know. I asked her if they were seeing each other."

Riley starts to laugh as well, but not nearly as bad as Char

"Sorry Chloe, but that's some funny shit. Hell no they are not seeing each other, that's my big sister were talking about. Plus that douche bag is still all hung up on you."

A smile spreads across my face and then I hear Char taking the phone back and yelling at him to shut his mouth.

"Sorry about that. I just fell into a fit of laughter and couldn't stop. That was pretty funny though. Now to clear things up, no Emma is not seeing Derrick…eww that is kind of gross. Besides she has enough shit on her plate to deal with. That being said there was some issues down in North Carolina with her husband and Riley asked her to come and stay up here. Since Derrick has the extra room we asked if she could stay there. I just wanted you to know."

"Oh, so she just moved in?" I ask.

"Umm, well not exactly. She actually moved in a few weeks ago, like the beginning of February."

"WHAT!" I scream. "She moved in months ago and you're just telling me now?"

"Relax Chloe, she's just living there. It's not like they are screwing each other. Not like it's any of your business."

I take in a deep breath and let it all out.

"I know I have no right to be freaking out like I am but it really sucks that a part of my life no longer exists. It still bothers me that we're not together. I've been doing really good about not mentioning him to anyone and trying to forget. It's just really hard Char."

Tears start to flood my vision and I can barely see the wall in front of me. I miss him so damn much.

"Well since you're already upset and crying I think I should mention one more detail."

"Oh god, now what?" I say.

"Please don't yell or scream in my ear again. I know for a fact that Derrick hasn't started a serious relationship with anyone since you broke up, but he has been spending a lot of time with the one junior partner from the firm. I know it's mainly for case purposes, but I thought you should know."

My throat has completely closed up at this point and I can't even utter a sound. I hit the end button on my phone and quick type a text to Char so she doesn't go into panic mode and fly out here.

Chloe – Sorry, I'm fine…just can't talk right now. I need some time to digest the fact that maybe he is moving on without me.

I toss the phone onto the couch and run into the bathroom. Spilling out my guts I cry into my toilet. This can't be happening. I thought he was my forever. This is all my fault and I'll never find my way back to him…no matter if I'm here in LA or back in Boston.

Fuck my life.

DERRICK

"I think we should celebrate!" Trisha shouts down the hallway as I come out of my office.

"Oh yeah, why is that?" I ask walking toward her.

"Well only because we have won the past five cases we worked on together." She says with a wink.

"Okay then. I completely agree with your point. What do you have in mind?" I ask wanting her to decide what we do.

The past few weeks we've been working together here at the firm or at my house after hours. Together we're a hard core team that seems to be quite invincible, but honestly that's all it is for me. I can tell her feelings are getting more intense and at times things may have gotten a little heated for us. I also know that there's no way I want to jeopardize my position at this firm for one night of sex.

"Why don't you come to my place tonight? You and Emma have been such great hosts to me over the past few weeks. I think it's only fair that I repay the favor." Trisha inches her body closer to where I stand so that she can reach out and touch my tie. She runs the fine silk through her fingers tips and with her closeness I can smell her perfume. Trisha is an exceptionally attractive woman, but I have to draw the line with her advances.

"Look I would like to celebrate our winning streak with you, but going back to your place isn't such a good idea." I try to tell her taking her hand from my tie and placing it back to her side.

"Come on Derrick. I promise I'll behave and we can make dinner together. No inappropriate actions on my part, I swear." She says as she makes a cross against her right breast.

She watches me as she trails her finger over her body and I have to blink ten times to regain my train of thought. I'm horny as hell and in need of a good fuck, but not with her.

"Fine. As long as you keep your hands to yourself."

She holds up her pinky and moves it closer to me. "Pinky swear." She says.

I accept the gesture knowing very well she is standing in front of me with her ankles crossed. I laugh at her deceit and figure what the hell. Damn this woman is sly.

"Let me go get my things and I'll meet you back out here in a few minutes."

Walking toward my office, I shake my head at her actions. There's no doubt in my mind that she is willing to take this relationship to a sexual level.

The image I now have in my mind is making it difficult to walk and I need to shut my door to adjust myself in my pants. My body is starving for the attention of a woman, but my heart is screaming at me to stop. I don't know how long I can let this go on. I think about Chloe every day. There are so many times I want to pick up the phone and call her, tell her I love her and beg her to quit her career and come back to me. But I know none of that will ever happen. Maybe I need to move on…has she?

This whole situation sucks. Part of me wants to wait forever for the one girl I love and can never have again and the rest of me wants to fuck my partner into next year. I look out the window at my view from my office. Everything I have worked so hard for up to this point has been to make me and Chloe happy. Now that she's gone I'm miserable. I know I'll never get her back because she is not coming back here to live.

Does that mean that I need to cut the apron strings and bite the bullet with Trisha? Damn it to hell, I say fuck it I'll see what happens. I'm a man in need of a good lay and I have a woman right here that is willing to give me just that.

That's it decision made. I'm throwing all discretions out the window and letting this night take me where I should go…here's to a night of celebration.

I pick up my stuff from my desk, shove it into my briefcase and walk out of my office closing the door behind me.

Trisha is standing by the elevators waiting for me with a grin on her face.

"Ready to go?" I ask.

"I was born ready to go." She replies and gives me a wink.

Damn it, I'm in for trouble tonight.

I follow Trisha to her house going through all the reasons why I shouldn't sleep with her and why I should. As a guy I feel like handing in my man card because as much as I need this as a release I also have two things that matter more than that…my job and my love.

We turn into a gated community and I see that she is telling the guy at the booth to allow me through as well. Driving past I give him a nod and follow her Mercedes around a bend and into a covered garage.

This place looks nice and it's not that far from the city.

I take in a deep breath and tell myself I can do this, even though I have no clue what I'm about to do. Trisha walks over to the door of my BMW and I get out following her to her condo.

Her place is nice, from what I can see. She keeps things neat and in order which is just how I am too.

For dinner we decide to grill out some chicken and vegetables. While I get the grill and food ready, Trisha pours herself a glass of wine and opens me a beer. Once again we work in sync with one another and barely have to utter a word.

A few times I can feel her hand graze my arm, my back and even at one point I could swear her hand was on my ass. With all of her touching I don't feel a spark, not a bolt of electricity or a hint of warmth when our bodies are close.

The weather is perfect outside so we choose to eat dinner out on her deck. After we're finished we decide to clean up and have another drink inside.

Trisha excuses herself for a minute and I take a seat on her white leather couch, beer in hand. Closing my eyes I play back my thoughts from earlier today. The need I have to be with a woman again, the love I have in my heart for a girl I'll never give it to and the concern that when I'm with Trisha I don't feel the vibe I always did with Chloe.

I hear her coming back out to the living room and feel the dip of the couch as she sits next to me. I open my eyes and see her sitting next to me holding her glass of wine.

"You look beat." She says in a soft voice.

"To tell you the truth I am. The past few weeks…no really months have been draining. I need a vacation from life for a bit."

"Well I can't help you with a real vacation, but I can help you relax." She purrs.

I scoot myself back into the couch to a taller seated position and she brings herself into my lap. Watching my reaction she brings her hands up to cup my face and slowly kisses my lips. My heart is pounding, my palms are sweating and the bulge in my pants is growing.

There's no doubt in my mind that I'm attracted to this girl. I deepen the kiss and pull her face closer to mine. She lets out a moan and grinds down on my growing erection. I can feel her hot pussy through my dress pants and I want so badly to flip her on her back and fuck her senseless.

"Derrick." She says breaking away from our kiss. "You have no idea how badly I want you right now. Please tell me you want me too."

I look into her beautiful blue eyes. As much as I want to tell her yes I want you too, I can't. This isn't right. I have to stop this now. I've been playing a tug a war with my feelings about this for far too long and I have to put an end to this now.

"Trisha, you're absolutely beautiful and if the rock hard cock in my pants is any indication of how turned on I am right now I would gladly take you back to your room. But, I can't. What we're doing is so wrong on so many levels. I'm sure I'll punch myself for this another day, but we can't do this. I'm sorry."

She slides off of my lap and lays her head on my shoulder.

"You're the first guy that has ever apologized for not wanting to sleep with me." She says with a giggle. "That Chloe girl, better get her ass in gear fast. If not, soon I won't take no for an answer."

I laugh at her comment and swing my arm around her.

"You are amazing. Do you know that?" I ask.

"Yeah? Well if I was so amazing you wouldn't have stopped us and we would be in my bedroom by now."

"That's not it Trisha and you know it. Yes Chloe is still a big part of me, but think about how things would be at work if we did sleep together and then things didn't work out."

"I guess you're right. Thanks for being such a good guy, Derrick. Chloe is one lucky lady." She says sitting up and walking toward her door.

I get up to follow her and pull her into a hug.

"I know this is lame to say, but we need to still be friends. You're a rock solid partner and I don't want to lose that."

"No worries there Derrick, I'm all yours at the office."

"Thanks Trisha, see you Monday." I tell her and walk out to my car.

Chapter 19
May 2013

CHLOE

I feel the sun shining through my bedroom window and the heat of the blaze is blaring against my face. Slowly I open my eyes.

Damn it! I grab my head that has grown its own heartbeat and is currently too heavy to hold up.

The memories of last night come flooding back to me. How could I have done this? Why would I allow myself to go that far knowing the only person I could ever love is not here with me?

I made a mistake and now I have to live with the regret and the pain that it will cause knowing I'll never be with Derrick again. Any chance I could have with him is gone, how will he ever trust me again? I know we are not together, but still my heart belongs to him…and only him.

Now awake, I sit up in my bed and toss my legs to the right. God I feel like shit, how much did I drink? How did I get home….oh no! Who brought me home?

I stand and stretch remembering exactly what happened last night. Oh shit, I'll have to face him. I look around my room for a t-shirt and I see a pile of clothes lying on the floor.

Fucking hell Chloe, these are not your clothes. I sit back down on the bed wearing only a tank top and boy shorts clutching my head in my hands.

Damn it! How could I have been so weak?

I mean he's extremely attractive, built like a fitness model, gorgeous bright green eyes that hide behind his rough exterior and dark…dark hair. Oh no I hung onto that hair like my life depended on it. Shit! Andrew Lock has been trying to get in my pants for over four months now and he almost had his chance last night.

It was all so wrong, it never should have happened. But it did and now I have to look him in those amazing green eyes soon, very soon.

I guess I could act like nothing happened. Can I? Will he?

With my eyes barely open I manage to make it into my bathroom to take a hot shower. I grab up my iPhone and listen to some music on my favorite Pandora channel hoping the music and the water will help me feel better I turn the temperature as hot as the pipes will allow. I take off my boy shorts and tank top and pull my hair down from my pony tail.

I step into the shower and emerge my entire body under the scolding hot water. It hurts so bad it feels good. A sound of relief moans past my lips as the pressure of my headache slowly releases. Reaching for the mango scented shampoo my body tenses as I feel a hand on my back and another closing the shower door.

My body turns to face a broad naked chest. I look up and see sparkling green eyes slowly being eaten away by black pupils screaming desire. He wraps his arms around me and pulls me into him so that we're skin to skin. This is too much. I've never touched another man like this other than Derrick. It feels so wrong.

I begin to say something, but before I can say a word his lips crash down onto mine. His lips are just as soft as I remember them from last night. He tastes like coffee and vanilla. I'm so consumed in this moment with him that any other thought is slipping from my grasp. As much as I want to believe this is wrong, right now it feels so right.

Andrew pulls me in closer to him so that my nipples are hard against his body. I moan at the feel of his skin against mine and my mouth opens. He doesn't take the invitation for granted and slides his tongue into my mouth. In this moment I throw out all morals and kiss him back. The feel of his mouth on mine and my tongue sliding against his is hypnotizing. I begin to lose my balance from my lack of control and he's picking me right back up against him. I tie my hands around his neck and enjoy the ride of lust we're traveling. His tongue leaves my mouth and begins to trail kisses along my jaw leading down to my collarbone.

Feelings I haven't felt in too long begin to surface and my pussy aches for him to touch me more. His hands begin to roam from my mid back down to my hips. He squeezes the hot flesh of my ass and I let out a moan of pleasure.

I pull away from the kiss gasping for a breath. His green eyes stare into mine and I take a step back. He reaches his arm out to grab mine and the feel of his rough hands pulls me out of my trance. The calluses he has on his throwing hand and fingers remind me so much of Derrick's when he played football in high school and college.

"Andrew we can't, I can't." I say, trying to avoid eye contact.

He touches my chin with two fingers and angles my face so that I'm looking up into his eyes.

"Chloe, we can do this. You can do this. I've wanted you for far too long. It's time to let go of the past and move forward with your life. Babe, I can be here for you."

Andrew says this with all the sincerity he can muster. I look up into his eyes. Between the pelting hot water and the heat looming between us my body and mind are taken into another world. As much as I love Derrick and wish things were different, Andrew is right. He is the one that is here for me right now. His body is the one that is touching mine.

I need to feel the way Andrew makes me feel. Derrick hasn't touched me, cared for me or loved me for months. Andrew is right, I need to let go of the past and move forward.

I can do this.

I want to do this.

"Oh god Andrew. You make me feel things that..."

He stops me right there and grab me up into his arms. Smashing his lips against mine our tongues join together in such an intimate way. I may not be able to have sex with this man right now, but I sure as hell want him to touch me.

"Please Andrew." I pant.

"I know babe, let me make you feel good."

He turns off the water and lifts me from the shower carrying me into my room. I can feel his hard erection pressing against my bottom and I'm getting wetter by the minute.

Andrew lays me down on the bed and my wet hair clings to my back. He takes his hands and runs his fingers from the top of my collar bone down to my toned stomach. The feel of his touch is creating goose bumps wherever he leaves a finger print.

Watching as his body is hovering over mine, I tremble with anticipation.

His lips and hands are all over my body. I look down and watch as he kisses each nipple taking them one at a time in his mouth. As he sucks and licks my breast the ache in my core increases. I can tell he is aroused as well and I feel the need to touch him.

As I stretch my arm to reach down for his length my phone begins to ring. I'm pulled out of my moment of lust and look down into his eyes.

Do I get up and answer the call? Do I ignore it and continue along with our moment of foreplay?

I choose the latter choice and reach to touch him again. This time it's not my cell that starts to ring, but my iPad chiming with an incoming Skype call.

Knowing there are only two people that have ever used Skype with me, I push Andrew away and lift my body into a seated position.

"I'm sorry, but I have to get this. It's an emergency if the call is coming through here."

"I understand, get to it." He says rubbing my arm.

I run into the bathroom and scoop up my robe, quickly putting it on I tie the strings in a knot. I make my way back out to my bedroom and grab the iPad moving into the living room for some privacy.

The Skype call was coming from Derrick's cell. I push the return call button and within on a few short rings I see his face.

"Derrick." I say barely in a whisper.

"Chloe, I'm sorry I'm calling you like this but you didn't answer the call I made to your cell." His voice is hoarse as if he is upset.

"Derrick, it's fine. What's wrong? Why are you out of breath?"

"Chloe, it's Char. She and Riley have been in a terrible accident."

My hand flies to my face as I gasp at his words. I think my heart just stopped.

DERRICK

"So are you sure about this man?" I ask looking at Riley while he paces my living room.

"Of course I'm sure dumbass." He replies running his fingers through his hair.

"Well if my opinion matters I think you have planned a wonderful evening little brother. Char is lucky to have you." Emma says in a sincere tone.

"Thanks a lot Emma, I feel so much better now." Riley says falling into the couch.

"I don't understand why you're so worked up about this. You two already act like a married couple. It's not like she's going to say no."

"Fuck you Derrick. Of course she isn't going to say no. I just want tonight to be perfect for her. She means the world to me and I want this to be a night she'll remember forever. This is the kind of thing she'll tell our kids and grandkids about. I don't want to blow it."

The poor guy has been sick to his stomach since Char left for the day at the spa with Angie and Ruthie. I know exactly how he feels. I felt the same way the day I was set to propose to Chloe. I just hope his night turns out better than mine did.

"Look why don't you run home, get some running gear on and head to the park with me and Emma. Maybe the fresh air and a good five miles will lift your spirits before the big night."

"Yeah, I'll be right back." Riley says and walks out the door with Manny in tow.

Emma and I just look at each other, shrug our shoulders and start to laugh.

Riley has got it bad for Char. They may have fallen fast for one another, but in the time they've been together they've grown so much as individuals. I'm happy for both of them. He just needs to calm the hell down before he gives himself a heart attack at a young age.

Thank god he has agreed to come along with us for a run. He can slam the pavement with his running shoes to release some of his nerves. Within a few hours Riley and Char will be a happily engaged couple and we'll all be meeting them for drinks afterwards at Callahan's Pub.

Emma and I make our way out to my car in the driveway waiting for Riley. Once we see him walking in the distance we both get in and buckle up.

"Let's hope this run clears his nerves. Otherwise I'll have to give him a valium before they leave." Emma says with a laugh.

"Nah, he'll be alright. He just needs to get through with it and everything will be fine."

Riley gets into the front seat and lets out a huge sigh.

"Thanks man, this was a good idea. I need to go for a good run to get this shit out of my system."

He pulls down on the rim of his hat and slaps me on the back.

Last one done with the five miles buys drinks for the other two tonight.

"Deal!" Emma and I shout in unison.

Once we get to the park the three of us shuffle out and line up along the trees. The plan is to run through the park and meet back here. I know for sure I can take Emma, but I'm not sure if I'll be able to out run Riley, surely not in the mood he is in right now.

"Okay assface, let's see if you can beat me. On your mark, get set, go." Riley shouts as we all take off in a sprint.

The next 45 minutes feel fucktasitic. I guess I needed this run more than I thought. The weather is perfect and it's just early enough that the sun isn't beating down on our bodies. By the time I get back to the car I'm dying of thirst. I pop open the truck and grab out three waters.

Riley comes walking around the car with a smirk on his face. It sucks that he beat me, but at least I'm not the one paying for us to get drunk tonight. I hand him bottle of water and watch as Emma approaches us.

"You both suck, don't even say a word."

Riley and I just look at each other, laugh and get in the car.

After we get home Riley makes his way back to his house to get ready for the big proposal, Emma says she has stuff she has to do and will catch up later which leaves me all by my lonesome.

Story of my fucking life lately, I just wish I could get her out of my mind. It's been four months since I've seen or spoken to her. I head up to my room and decide to take a shower and a nap before I have to get ready to meet up with the crew at the pub.

I wake up from my nap to a banging on my bedroom door.

What the fuck.

I glance over at my alarm clock and I see it's 6:30.

Shit I never sleep that long during the day.

I get out of bed and head over to the door. As I open it Emma falls into me crying.

"Emma, what's wrong. Why are your crying?"

"Oh my god Derrick, hurry get dressed we have to go." She says between sobs.

"Slow down Emma, what's going on?"

"It's Char. There was an accident. We need to go to her. Now!"

"Okay, okay Emma. Let me get dressed and we will go."

"Oh Derrick, you have to call Chloe. Teresa and Bryce are on their way to the hospital."

Fuck! I have to call Chloe.

While I attempt to throw on a tee-shirt and shorts I dial Chloe's cell.

"Damn it, she's not answering."

"You have to keep trying. She has to pick up eventually." Emma yells at me.

"Go into the office and grab my briefcase. I'll Skype her."

Emma comes back into my room and I'm dressed ready to go. I sit down on my bed and pull up the Skype app on my iPad. I hoover over her picture and within two seconds find the balls to push it.

The line chimes a few times and finally I see her face on the screen.

"Derrick." She says in a whisper.

"Chloe, I'm sorry I'm calling you like this but you didn't answer the call I made to your cell."

"Derrick, it's fine. What's wrong? Why are you upset?"

"Chloe, it's Char. She and Riley have been in a terrible accident."

Chapter 20

CHLOE

Getting a flight back to Boston was the easy part. It was getting me up off the floor after Derrick told me the news. I felt numb from my head to my toes. Not only was I in a state of shock, but I wanted to trade places with Char more than anything.

As soon as I ended the Skype call I looked into the hallway and saw Andrew standing there. He didn't hesitate for a second and walked right over to me. Scooping me up into his arms he sat us down on the couch and helped me book my flight. I'm glad I wasn't completely alone when I got the news. It helped a lot having him there, but leaving him in LA was hard. I think more on him than me. He offered to fly back to Boston with me, but I told him that it would be best for me to go back home alone.

Seeing my baby sister hurting is going to be hard, but seeing Derrick and not talking to him will be next to impossible.

I'm still in shock and I hate that it's going to take me eight hours to get home. My poor baby sister, why her. She's never done a hurtful thing to anyone in her life. Char would rip the shirt off her back to help a stranger. She has to be okay. I'm a ball of nerves and no one has called me since I text mom my flight itinerary. She said someone would be there to pick me up, but she wasn't sure who. I told her not to worry about sending me a ride. I could just grab a cab to the hospital. Everyone in Boston is probably a frantic mess and the last thing I want is for someone to leave to come and get me.

I lean forward and place my head in my hands. I have a ball of tissues in one and my cell in the other. My head is pounding either from the alcohol I drank last night or all the crying I've done this morning. I could really use a cup of coffee and some pain medicine to help curb this headache. Looking up I see that there's a Starbucks near the gate. I glance at the time on my iPhone and see that I still have an hour till they will start boarding our plane. Since I have plenty of time I make my way over to get in my caffeine fix and then to the newsstand for some Ibuprofen.

I get to the gate and take a seat with my hot coffee, muffin and bottle of water. This should help at least I hope it will. I feel my phone vibrate and I see I have a text from mom. I slide the lock screen and when I read the message it's actually from Derrick.

Mom – Chloe it's Derrick. Teresa isn't in any shape to call you so I thought I would just send a text through her phone. Char's not good Chloe, things aren't looking good.

My breath catches and I almost choke on the muffin I just put in my mouth. I don't know how to respond, to be honest I don't want to talk about this over a text message.

After thinking it over a few minutes I gather up the courage to call Derrick's cell. I don't know why he was using mom's cell to begin with, but with her being so upset I really don't want to call her phone and bother her. I make my way over to a corner in the room and dial his number.

"Chloe hey, sorry about the text I just don't know what to do right now."

I start crying hearing his voice.

"I'm trying to get home as soon as I can. My flight doesn't leave for another half hour. Please tell me she'll be okay till then?"

"I don't know what is going to happen Chloe. The truck hit her side of the car and broke just about every bone on the right side of her body. She has a head injury that they are monitoring closely hoping that blood doesn't sit on her brain."

"Oh god Derrick, why Char?"

By now I'm sobbing so hard people are starting to stare at me from the gate. I wipe my tears with the sleeve of my sweatshirt and try to focus on the conversation.

"Chloe don't. Just get here and be with her. I can't talk now, but I'll call if anything changes."

"Okay Thanks Derrick."

And the line goes dead. He doesn't say bye or get here safe or anything.

Char is just as much a sister to him and she is mine. I know that this is killing him.

I go back over to the chair I was sitting in before and attempt to wipe my face with the tissues I brought with me. I only have a few more minutes till we will start to board so I finish up my coffee. I lean back in the rock hard airport chair and think how my life has gotten to this point and how I pushed everyone away including him.

Someone once told me everyone has a special someone they are meant to be with forever. A man who will be my world, my partner in life, and the one person I can grow old with and always be at my side.

Maybe I never found that right person to begin with.

No! That can't be right. I had my person and I was too wrapped up in my own little bubble to realize what was right in front of me.

He was the one.

He was my forever.

I screwed it up over my own damn selfish needs.

I thought I had chosen the path in life that was best for me, but I seem to have lost my soul mate along the way.

Waiting to board a plane back to Boston, I sit here wondering if I made the right choices in life. Did I follow the path that would take me in the right direction? Could I have done something different that would change the outcomes I am faced with right now?

I haven't seen or spoken to him in four months. Four long, torturous months dealing with what I did to us and our happily ever after. I know I'll run into him soon, but when I do I'm not sure how he'll react. He can accept me in an embrace or turn the corner and run the other way.

What did I do?

The choices I made changed my life in only a short period of time and I fear I may have lost him forever.

At one time he was all I ever knew. The two of us were so in sync with the other no force field could tear us apart. I can hear him whisper in my ear. "Chloe you and I will stand the test of time because I was touched by you and only you."

I, Chloe Taylor, am faced with a decision I may not like myself for in the next few hours. Only time will tell what is meant to be and for now I have a much bigger weight on my plate than that of my love life.

DERRICK

After getting off the Skype call with Chloe, Emma and I make our way over to the hospital. The ER is packed, most likely because it's a Saturday, but thankfully we're able to spot Bryce and Teresa right away.

Taking Emma's hand we run over to them and Bryce releases Teresa from his grasp as she clings onto both Emma and I. Bryce tries to explain to us the little detail they know while Teresa cries into Emma's shoulder. There isn't much news on either Riley or Charlie other than she was rushed straight into the O.R. for immediate surgery. My heart falls to the floor and I feel the need to sit down.

Of all days, the day Riley was meant to propose to Charlie. This was supposed to be the happiest day of her life and they never made it to that point. I feel tears begin to cloud my vision and an ache starts to rip through my heart. I've known Charlie as my little sister for too long. She has to be okay. She needs to pull through and marry that dumbass Riley.

The four of us take a seat until we hear word from a doctor.

About an hour later we still have not heard the condition of either family member and we're all beginning to worry more and more. My parents show up and I'm grateful for their support. It means a lot for them to be here with a huge part of my family, regardless if Chloe and I are together or not.

Another hour goes by and the six of us are on pins and needles waiting to hear from a nurse or a doctor.

Emma decides to take a walk since the waiting is getting to her. My mom offers to go with her and get some coffee from the cafeteria. Trying to pry Teresa from her seat is a feat, but eventually the girls get her to go along.

We sit in silence for a few minutes. Now that they are gone I feel it's a good time to ask Bryce if he knows actually what happened.

"What details did the police give you about the accident?" I ask moving over to the seat next to him and my dad.

"They didn't give us much when they called and no one has talked to us since we got here. It seems that they were at a four way stop and when Riley pulled out to go a truck plowed through the sign without stopping. The other driver was going about 40-45 mph and hit Char's side of the car. That's all we know."

"This is fucking ridiculous. Someone has to tell us more. They could both be dead right now for all we know." I say punching the chair next to me.

"Derrick Mason Peters, don't talk like that!" My mom shouts.

"Damn it mom, someone has to know something. This isn't right. What if one of them needs us? We can't help them from out here."

I'm trying to remain calm, but two of my best friends are hurt and there's nothing I can do about it.

"Here take this and let's go walk outside." Emma says.

I know she is just as upset as I am, my god it's her brother in there. To keep the peace I take the cup of coffee from her and follow her outside.

Emma is texting like crazy on her phone and I have no clue who the hell she could be talking to. I'm certain it's not her husband Keith and the rest of us are here. Hmm that's a conversation for a later time I guess.

We sit out on the curb for what feels like forever and eventually Bryce comes out to get us.

"We just spoke to the doctor that saw Riley and Char when the ambulance brought them into the ER."

"Thank fuck, it's about time. What did they say?"

Tears start to glaze his eyes and a lump grows in my throat.

"Well the good news is that Riley is okay. He has a broken humerus, collar bone and a few cuts from the windshield breaking, but we can go see him in a few minutes."

Emma lets out a sigh and I know a huge weight has been lifted from her chest, but Charlie …what about Charlie?

"Okay so if that's the good news, what did they say about Charlie?" I ask.

Bryce's face is now wet with tears and I can only hope for the best.

"She's still in surgery. She has broken majority of her bones on the right side and has a severe head injury. Even after surgery it will be difficult to know what will happen for a few days. She needs to wake up and come back to us. Then we can help her heal with the rest of her injuries."

Seeing this grown man cry and hear Emma crying behind me make the dam burst. The tears fall fast down my face and in my emotion state I grab onto Bryce and Emma.

Charlie isn't just Chloe's sister. This family isn't just Chloe's, they are mine too. I can't lose Charlie. She's my best friend. She has helped me get through some of the hardest times of my life. I can't live without my Charlie…I have to be here for her just as she has always been here for me.

The three of us pull away from our group hug and make our way back into the ER. We'll be able to go up to Riley's room now so I say a silent prayer following the nurse and my family up to see the only brother I have ever really known.

Chapter 21

CHLOE

After a long ass flight I'm finally going to be setting foot into my home town of Boston, Massachusetts. Once I got on the plane the flight wasn't so bad. My head was feeling a bit better, but I knew I needed to catch up on some sleep. I remove my sweatshirt from my bag and place it against the window. Since I'll be here for awhile I figure I might as well take a nap. I know my mind will be racing as soon as I land, so the more sleep I can get now the better.

I'm jolted awake when the plane lands on the runway. Rubbing my sleepy eyes I try to focus on my watch to see the time. It's already eight o'clock here on the east coast and the sky is getting darker as the sun sets. I always loved to watch the sun setting at Pier Park and on the boat with Derrick. The memories of our times together make me happy, but with everything going on I wish I had a reason to smile right about now.

The thought of what I'm about to walk into scares me. As much as I wish it were me in that hospital, it really is Char. I can't imagine my life without my baby sister in it and I'm so scared to find out what's going on once I get there. Now that the plane is taxing the run way I turn my phone back on to see if I have any missed calls or text messages.

My palms begin to sweat and my heart starts to become more rapid. Finally a text alert pops on the screen from a number I don't recognize.

326-555-1212 – Pete, Chris and Tony will pick you up at the airport on their way to the hospital

Okay then, so the Taylor & Sons Contracting crew is coming to get me, better than hailing a cab…I guess. I have known Pete, Chris and Tony pretty much most of my teenage to adult life. Not like they are much older than me and Char, but when they started working for daddy they instantly became an extended part of our family. They are great guys and always had our backs if we needed them. I know Char said that Derrick had been hanging out with Riley and Pete a lot over the past few months so I hope him coming to get me isn't going to be awkward. He really is a nice guy, not quite sure why he's still single ….hmm that is an interesting thought though. Chris and Tony have both been married for years and have a few kids each so I 'm sure they haven't been hitting up the pubs with the guys lately.

Oh well, I'm not here to see them. I need to see my sister and if they're my ride to where she is, then I'll suck it up with a smile on my face. I put my iPhone back into my purse and pull my sweatshirt over my head. The line down the main aisle of the plane slowly starts to move. I kindly wait my turn and when the guy next to me exits our row I make my move. I walk out of the plane into the tunnel and try not to breath in the stale air of the airport.

When I exit the tunnel I see all three men standing there waiting. Tony has his hands tucked into his washed out jeans with a white tee-shirt and backwards baseball cap. Chris is wearing darker jeans with a navy blue Red Sox tee arms crossed and a pout on his face. Then there's Pete, he eyes me immediately and starts walking my way. He too is wearing a pair of faded jeans with a black tee-shirt.

I approach my entourage and give them all a big hug without saying a word. Looking into their eyes I can see the sadness knowing that a member of the Taylor family is hurt.

The guys walk us to Pete's truck and they insist I sit up front. Chris takes my suitcase and throws it in the back while Tony opens the passenger side door for me. I appreciate the chivalry of the guys, but it makes me even more nervous that they are treating me like glass. The ride to the hospital we're all silent. In fact I don't think any of us have said a word since I arrived.

My chest begins to tighten, more so than it has, and I feel the need to take a deep breath. Pete must sense my sudden unease and he looks in my direction grabbing for my hand. He rubs his thumb back in forth along my palm and quietly reassures me that everything will be okay.

I look over in his direction and a small smile appears on his face. As much as I want his gesture to make me feel better and believe Char will be okay, I need to be by her side to know for sure. Thanking Pete with a nod of my head I reposition myself, take my hand back and lean into the soft leather seat of his truck.

We pull into Massachusetts General Hospital and my heart plummets to my feet. My entire body feels numb and the anxiety of what awaits us inside scares me.

Pete turns off the truck and turns to face me.

"Chloe, are you okay to get out and walk to the door? You look like you're about to pass out." He asks.

My body is shaking in fear. His warm hand touches my shoulder and a chill runs through me.

"We'll walk right in with you sugar." Tony says.

"Yeah, I'll even hold your hand if it will make you feel better." Chris tells me.

I turn and look at the three men standing outside the door and small sense of relief fills me. Although they are not immediate family, they're all still here to show support in our time of need. I grab for Chris's hand and he helps me out of the truck. I reach for my purse and hop down onto the black macadam. Pete comes around to my other side and grabs my left hand. Walking to the door of MGH I have these three strong men standing by my side. I just wish their strength was enough to erase this day from ever happening. .

DERRICK

As soon as Riley was taken to a room the six of us started our journey up to the fourth floor of Massachusetts General Hospital. The nurses suggested that only two of us should go in at a time and that we needed to keep him calm and relaxed so that he can rest.

Emma and Teresa were the first two to go in to see him and assured me they wouldn't stay more than a half an hour. I wanted to be there for him, but having his sister and soon to be mother-in-law by his side seemed like a better choice. I walked over to the window in the waiting area and realized that half of the day had already passed. Looking at my watch I couldn't believe it was four o'clock in the afternoon. We had been sitting around in the ER most of the day. Now we continue to wait to see Riley, two at a time, and hear word from the doctors once Charlie is out of surgery.

I feel a warm hand touch my shoulder and turn to see it's my mom.

"Honey, dad and I are going to go grab something to eat. Would you like to come with us? Bryce said he'll call as soon as he hears anything about Char."

Her voice is so soft, so sweet and so caring. I'm so grateful to have both of my parents in my life. There isn't two other people in the whole world who could have taught me more about support and love than my parents.

"Nah, I'm good mom. I want to be here when Charlie gets out of surgery." I tell her.

"Derrick, don't be surprised if they don't let you in to see her. I know you're close, but you're not her immediate family." She says rubbing her hand up and down my back for support.

"There's no need to worry about that." Bryce says walking over toward the window. "All three of you are considered to be Char's immediately family and I'll make certain each of you are able to go in and see her. She needs to hear all of us telling her to get her ass up."

"Thanks Bryce that means a lot…to all of us."

"Oh that is a relief, thank you Bryce. Okay Derrick, dad and I are going to leave for a bit and will be back later tonight. Do you want us to bring anything back for you guys?"

"No thanks mom. I'll call you if we hear anything."

I give both my parents a hug and kiss goodbye and then retreat back to the uncomfortable chairs in the waiting room.

Thirty minutes later Emma and Teresa walk out of the doors, both of their faces stained with tears. Bryce and I stand and walk toward them.

"How is he?" I ask.

"He looks like shit, but says he's just in a bit of pain." Emma says.

"He's really beating himself up over this Derrick. You need to go in there and tell him this isn't his fault. He was knocked out with the impact and feels he should have been able to protect Char."

Tears pour from Teresa's eyes and Bryce pulls her into a quick embrace.

Emma pulls me to the side. "Derrick I know you and Riley are close, but I do know him a bit better. Teresa wasn't joking when she said he was taking this hard. Char is his whole world. I've never seen him care about anyone as much as he does with her. We need to keep him focused on getting himself better and not about her. I know it's a lot to ask but can you do that for him? Help him not think about her?"

"Emma do you realize what you're asking me to do? Those two have been attached by the hip since the moment they met. They have a magnetic pull and without the other they are a fucking mess. How do you suppose I help him not think about her?"

"I don't know Derrick, but I do know my brother. If he has his way he'll unhook every cord attached to him and march his way up to the ICU."

"I can't promise you anything Emma, but I'll stay by his side. Are you going to come back in with me?"

"No, I'm going to run home. I need to shower and change. Do you want me to bring you anything back?"

"Nah, I'm good thanks Emma. My parents just left to go get something to eat. I'll see you guys when you get back."

Emma walks over to the chairs and picks up her things. Before she leaves she gives a hug to both Bryce and Teresa. As she walks past me she pats me on the shoulder and mouths, *thank you.*

I look over to Bryce and Teresa who are sitting on a loveseat. Bryce has his head in his hands and Teresa is sitting back against the cushions with her eyes closed. I want to go in to see Riley, but I also want to be out here when the doctors come out to talk to them.

Teresa opens her eyes and sees me pacing.

"Derrick, why don't you go on in?" She asks.

"I want to be here when they come to talk to you. I don't want to miss seeing her."

"Honey, I promise I'll come in and get you as soon as they come out. You have to know that she won't be awake right away anyhow. Go in and talk to Riley, he needs you right now."

With that, I nod my head and make my way over to the two large doors. I push the button for them to open and I walk around the hallway till I find room 1030.

I clench my fists and feel my palms begin to sweat as I enter his room. When I walk around the curtain I see Riley is asleep. Emma was right, he does look like shit.

His head is wrapped in a white bandage and a few strands of his hair are poking through the top. I walk over to the side of his bed and can see that blood has stained his face, neck and chest area. His arm and shoulder are in an odd looking cast that is supported with a rod that is attached to somewhere on his body near his right side.

I still can't believe this is happening. It's like a fucking nightmare. I know my friend needs me and will probably be a wreck when he wakes from his nap. I decide to take a seat in his room and wait it out till either he wakes up or Teresa comes in to give me some news.

Chapter 22

CHLOE

Once inside the main doors of the hospital Tony walks over to the information booth to see where Riley and Char are within this huge place. I've never had the need to go to the hospital in my entire life, just lucky I guess. Tony walks back over to us and I watch his eyes as they glance down to my hands. Both Pete and Chris are still hanging on to me for dear life and I just smile at the expression on Tony's face.

"You would think these two douche bags were your only life line Chloe." Tony says with a smirk.

"Well if this is the lifeline I need to survive, I think I'll just deal." I tell him while looking back n forth between these two handsome men on either side of me.

Pete looks me right in the eyes and squeezes my hand. "You ready to do this doll?"

"As much as I would like to say no, I think we better get up there. Lead the way Tony." I say lifting my arms to get Chris and Pete moving.

Accompanied by the three amigos we get into the elevator and Chris hits the #4 button. My heart rate increases as the elevator lifts up to the fourth floor. When the doors open I can see the visitors waiting area. We get off the elevator and Chris leads up around the corner through a set of wooden doors. Just pass the entrance is another room where I see mom, dad, Rose, Bud and Derrick holding hands with some girl.

Oh god. Not only am I about to panic about what may be going on with my sister, but I have to stand here and watch Derrick and his girlfriend. Okay breathe Chloe, breathe….in and out…in and out.

"Hey, you okay Chloe?" Pete asks.

I shake my head no and he leads me back out the doors and to the restroom. Without even hesitating he opens the women's door and follows me. He escorts me over to the sinks and splashes some water into a paper towel.

"Here take this and wipe your face. You need to calm down your breathing before you have a panic attack. And believe me I've been on drugs for years for those fuckers."

I have no clue why he's doing this, but I listen as he talks and calm myself down.

"I know you're freaked out about Char, but she'll be fine. You two girls are the biggest fighters in Boston, you can get through anything." He tells me with a big smile and his blue eyes sparkling.

"Pete it's not that. I mean it's not Char. Well yeah I'm a nut case with everything that happened today, but seeing Derrick here with his girlfriend. Damn it, why did he have to bring her here. Was she close with Char? Is that why she's here?"

Pete looks at me like I've grown a second head.

"Chloe, what the hell are you talking about. Of all people I should know if Derrick has a girlfriend, which he doesn't. Who are you talking about? The only girls out there are your mom, his mom and Emma. And she sure as hell is not Derrick's."

Oh my god Emma, I didn't even think about her. I look up at Pete and feel like a complete ass.

"I've been so consumed about Char, I totally forgot about Riley. Emma is Riley's sister and I…I thought she was with Derrick. I mean when we walked in there, I saw…well they were holding hands and ugh, I'm a stupid idiot."

Pete takes the ripped up paper towel I've been destroying from my hands and throws it in the trash. Lifting my chin with his fingers he makes me look him straight in the eye.

"Look Chloe, I've know Derrick as long as I've known you. The two of you are perfect for one another. Just get your shit worked out because honestly I'm sick of hearing him bitch like a girl about you. He loves you and you love him. Deal with it and make it work. Capice?"

I laugh at the tone Pete is using and the words he says. He's totally right, I do love Derrick and need to find a way to make this work. I just hope it isn't too late.

"Capice." I respond.

"Okay then, get yourself cleaned up and meet us back out in the waiting room." He tells me with a stern voice and points his finger at me as if to scold me.

And with that Pete walks out of the women's restroom and I plan to do exactly as he says. He just told me that Derrick still loves me.

With all the pain I feel about what Char is going through, I still feel a sense of happiness knowing that Derrick still loves me.

I quickly splash water on my face and dry my eyes to remove the melting mascara. Now that I look presentable I take a deep breath and head out of the restroom and into the room that holds our families.

As soon as I walk through the doors my parents stand and walk over to me. Mom is the first to get within a close enough range to grab a hold of me and she does just that. Right behind her is dad and as a family we all begin to cry. The three of us hold one another so tightly that I begin to struggle for a breath. I loosen my hold from mom and dad soon follows suit.

"Hey kiddo, glad you could get here so quickly. We just wish it was under different circumstances." Dad says.

"I know. Me too." I reply.

Mom wipes at her eyes and does the same for me giving me a kiss on the nose.

"Have you guys heard anything more about Char or Riley? I feel like such an ass. With all my worry focused on Char I completely forgot to ask about Riley."

"Riley is a bit banged up and has a broken humerus and collar bone, but other than that he's just beating himself up about the whole thing. Rose and I were just in to sit with him for a bit, but they wanted to get him in for a cat scan so we had to leave." Mom tells me while playing with my hair.

She always has a need to do something with her hands when she is nervous. Thankfully I love to have my hair played with when I'm scared. We are a perfect match right now.

"Well that's good, but what about Char? Is she okay? I mean I know she isn't okay right now, but is she out of surgery yet?"

"She's out of surgery and they've been able to stop the bleeding on her brain. They'll have to do a bit of restructuring to her right arm and leg once she is out of the coma they placed her in, but for right now all we can do is wait for her to wake up." Dad says rubbing his hands up and down my back.

My hand flies to my mouth as I gasp for air.

"She's gonna wake up though, right?"

The tears begin to fall from my cheeks and the fear of losing my little sister increases the longer my parents take to respond to my question.

"We don't know yet kiddo."

I move away from my parent in need of a seat. My legs begin to feel weak and I don't know how much longer they'll be able to support me. Once I sit, I throw my head into my hands and begin to sob.

Char has to wake up. She has to be okay. Char is the rock that holds us all together. She is the one that makes us a better family.

DERRICK

This waiting around shit fucking sucks and I don't know how much more patient I can be. I know that there are hundreds of other patients in this hospital, but how hard is it for one nurse or doctor to let us know how Char's surgery is going?

I've been sitting in Riley's room for the past two hours and he's knocked out. If it weren't for the damn beeping of the machines I'd think the guy was dead. Oh wait, I shouldn't even think that. I'm grateful he's alive and breathing. Fuck this whole day is turning me into a nut case.

I know when he wakes up he's going to go off the grid and if it were me I would do the same damn thing.

God if it were me and Chloe in this situation I'd be going bat shit crazy trying to get out of this bed and up to find her. There's no way I could lay here knowing she was somewhere else in pain and I couldn't help her heal with my touch.

Fucking shit, what am I even thinking? Chloe and I will never even be together again to get us in a situation like this.

I lean forward on my legs and put my head in my hands. Feeling the need to relieve some pressure I run my fingers through my hair and pull.

A knock on the door jolts me from my mood of irritation. I look up and see my mom standing in the door way. She walks toward me and grabs for me to stand. Pulling me out of my chair she silently walks me out of Riley's room and into the hallway.

Once we're in the hallway, she moves me to turn and face her.

"Dad and I just got back a few minutes ago and I wanted to come in and see how you were holding up. The doctors just came out to talk to Teresa and Bryce about Char. Why don't you come on out and hear what they had to say. Then I suggest you go home and get a shower and something to eat. You look like you could use a recharge."

"Thanks mom, if I didn't already feel like shit, I sure do now."

She gives me a smile that warms my heart and I wrap an arm around her shoulders as we walk out of the hallway and back into the waiting room. Walking into the room I see Teresa and Bryce stand and walk toward us.

They both have a calm expression on their faces which is hard to read. I don't know if what they are about to tell me is going to be good or bad. I clench my fists to my side and hope for the best.

"Well, let me have it. How is she?" I ask.

Bryce wraps Teresa into his side and she puts her hand to her mouth. Tears fall from both of their faces and I feel the urgent need to sit. This can't be good.

"She is out of surgery and will remain in the ICU till they know more about her condition. When she went into surgery there were a lot of things going wrong at once, but they had to focus on what was important first." Bryce says.

"So what does that mean, did they fix what's wrong with her? Will she be okay? Can we see her?" I ask stumbling over my words.

"Her head injury was pretty intense and that was their main concern. They found the area that was causing blood to sit on a section of her brain and they were able to stop it." Bryce says.

"Thank god." Teresa chimes in and reaches for my hand. "She needs our thoughts and prayers more than anything else right now. They said immediate family can go up to see her in a few hours. They want to monitor her pretty closely first. The nurse said she'll come down and let us know as soon as we can go up."

I look between the two people that love Charlie more than their own lives. This is a hard pill for all of us to swallow. I can't imagine how much this is hurting them.

"I don't know what to say or do. I feel lost and helpless right now."

"Derrick there's nothing you could do to prevent this and nothing you can do right now but pray for our Char."

I nod my head in agreement. "Well I think I'm going to go home and get a shower. I know Emma will be back soon to keep an eye out for Riley, but till then will you go in and keep him company mom?"

"Of course we will son, he's an important part of this family and we need him to get better too." She says.

"While I'm over at the house, I'll check in on Manny and make sure he has food and water. Thank god for the doggy door Char insisted Riley install last week. The poor dog would be pissing all over the place."

"Good thinking." Bryce says.

"Do either of you need anything while I'm out?"

"No we're good. Chloe and the guys should be here in a few hours and by then I hope we can go up and see her." Teresa says.

"Okay, call me if anything changes with Charlie or Riley."

"Will do Derrick, be safe."

"Always." I reply and walk out of the room heading home.

On my way to the house I think of how quickly life can change. How in a split second someone you love can be taken away. I try to remember the last thing I said to either of them and a draw a blank. I know that both of them know how important they are to me and I never go a day without telling them how much I appreciate their friendship.

My mind wonders back to the thoughts of what I would do if it were Chloe in the ICU. That girl was my life before I even knew she meant the world to me. Being apart from her for the past few months has been torture. I miss her. I love her. I can't stand another day being apart from her. But I don't know if we could ever make it work. We tried and we failed once before. Who's to say if we did try again it would work?

Fucking hell, what am I even thinking? I don't even know how she feels. For all I know she has already moved on and hasn't wasted a second of her time thinking about me.

This sucks and all I know is that I still love Chloe. I need to get her back and I need to never let her go again.

Chapter 23

CHLOE

Shortly after I arrive at the hospital and hear the news of Char I'm introduced to Emma. I still feel like a jackass for assuming she was dating Derrick, but now that I've met her I feel a bit better. There's a lot that I need to get reacquainted with if I'll be moving back to Boston.

God, I haven't even thought about where I'll live. I mean I own a house with Derrick, but that doesn't mean I can just move back in…does it? Shit I need to think some things through and fast.

Now that the whole crew is here we have pretty much taken over the family waiting area. I look around at all the people that are here showing their love and support for my sister and Riley. I haven't gone over to say hello to Rose and Bud yet though I'm feeling kind of guilty. Not for fear of rejection, but because Derrick is now sitting between them and Emma has found a home next to Rose.

Knowing that Derrick still loves me is the best feeling in the world, but I still feel a bit awkward. A few times we've caught one another looking in the other's direction. It's funny how we've spent majority of our lives together and now it's as if we're complete strangers. I want to be able to run over to him and sit on his lap. I want him to be the one to comfort me and me to be there for him. It's a sticky situation we're in and I want more than anything to talk to him alone.

I need to tell him that there's a huge possibility that I'll be moving back here to Boston. In fact my final interview is this coming Monday at the Red Sox and Orioles game. My family will be thrilled to know that I'll be so close again, but is it the right time to tell them? Everyone is so consumed with the fear of what will happen to Char. Would me telling them my news make them feel better? I wish I knew the answers so I could break the silence in the room. It's making me a little nervous.

Pete begins to stand and I see him move over to Emma out of the corner of my eye. She too gets up from her chair and they walk over to Derrick. The three of them walk toward us and my heart begins to beat at an uncontrollable speed. I don't know why but seeing him and having him so near has my nerves and heart racing.

Derrick extends his hand to me and I look up at him.

"We're going to go grab some coffee. Do you want to join us?" He asks me.

Hearing his voice and having him talk to me gives me goose bumps down my arms and butterflies in my stomach. It amazes me how much his body still effects mine. I grab his hand and allow him to help me from my seat. I give him a smile and nod my head. He never lets go of my hand and I don't try for second to pull it away.

I can feel the warmth from his touch spread through my entire body and I feel as though I'm on fire. I have missed this, I've missed him.

I turn and look at my parents telling them to call my cell if they hear anything about Char or Riley. Derrick pulls me forward and I look into his baby blues. He's smiling at me and my heart melts.

"So where we going?" I ask.

"Well Pete and I are going for a walk outside to get some fresh air." Emma says. "And we both agreed that you and Derrick need a chance to talk. The sexual tension is thick enough to get your parents in the mood for a little wam bam thank ya mam up there."

"Fuck Emma, that's just gross." Derrick says. "But I do agree that we should talk. You wanna go to the cafeteria and grab some coffee?"

"Yeah."I reply. My throat feels like there's a million cotton balls lodged in there and I'm feeling nervous to be alone with Derrick.

Emma and Pete follow us down to the elevator, but stay on when we get off on the second floor.

We walk in silence to the cafeteria our hands still interlocked the entire way.

So many thoughts and questions are racing through my mind. I have no clue how Derrick feels about any of this. We left one another on such emotional terms and haven't spoken a word to one another in months. Even though Pete said Derrick still loves me, what if he isn't still *in love* with me anymore?

Can four months of being apart erase the love and passion we shared for so long? Choosing my career over Derrick was a difficult decision, but look at where it has lead me, right back to him.

I have heard it over and over again, everything happens for a reason. And even Char told me that if Derrick and I were meant to be together, we'd find our way back to each other.

I think we just did. But wait, did he find someone else while I was gone…did he date? Oh god how will I explain things with me and

Andrew to him? I can't keep it a secret. I mean, even though we were never intimate I still owe him an explanation…right?

I glance over at him as we walk through the cafeteria doors and my heart skips a beat. I know that I'm still totally in love with him. Not even the past few months could take that away from me. I miss looking into those baby blue eyes, running my fingers through his soft brown hair and wake up every morning to his touch.

In some ways I feel like nothing has changed between us, but I know better than that. A lot has changed. Where do we go from here?

DERRICK

If someone would have told me that I would have the worst and best day of my life today I probably would have stayed in bed waiting for the best part to come find me.

Seeing Chloe after all of these months has my heart racing and my mind spinning with the memories of how we used to be happy. I can shut my eyes and play back every moment we've spent together. I'm so in love with this girl that I rightfully deserve to have my man card revoked.

If only it were that easy. For the past four months I walked around in a fog trying to figure out how I would move on with my life after losing Chloe. I see how happy Charlie and Riley were every day I was with them and it ripped my heart apart. I don't mean to be a dick or anything, but there's only so much hugging and kissing a guy can take when he's not the one getting the action.

There have been a few times that Emma and I were over at their house for dinner or a movie or just to hang out and we cut the night short because of their public displays of affection. I really am happy for my two best friends, but when you are depressed and missing the one you love that kind of scene is not where you want to be for too long.

I take another look over in Chloe's direction and she is sitting between her parents with her head resting on Bryce's shoulder. Her mom has her hand wrapped around Chloe's arm and is running her nails up and down it for comfort I'm sure. I can't help but watch her from the short distance we are sitting apart. So much as happened today, yet my mind is focused on her. I have this unnerving need to pick her up and sit her on my lap. I want to be the one to soothe her worries, to make her feel better and to tell her it will all be okay. A few times we've made eye contact and just as quickly as our eyes meet, they drifted back apart. I wish I knew what was on her mind when she looks at me.

I think it's great that she jumped on a plane and came out here to be with our families. Of course she did, Char is her sister, but I wonder what she had to leave behind to be here. Her career is one of the most important things in her life. So important she chose that over our relationship. I still dwell on the memories of that day. There's a pain from that day that I don't think will ever go away.

I never thought I'd have to say goodbye to the love of my life and I sure as hell don't want to do it again. How long will Chloe be here in Boston? I wonder if she's able to stay here for a day, two days a week maybe. When does she have to be back out in LA? I know how busy life was out there for her and I'm sure things have only gotten more intense with her new position.

She's been traveling the past few days with March Madness and from the looks of ESPN Live they've already replaced her position. I hate not knowing what she's doing and watching from a far. It kills me that there's this awkwardness between us. We've been friends most of our lives but the best years together with her have been those that we were a couple. I keep fighting the need to get up and touch her, but now isn't the time or place.

I wonder if she found someone else. Maybe there's someone in LA that makes her feel things I couldn't because we lived too far apart. I don't even think I want to know if she did. It would seriously crush me to know if she was seeing someone else. Great now I feel like a hypocrite. Just a few days ago I had another girls tongue down my throat and now I'm sitting here getting pissed off thinking Chloe could have been doing the same thing with some guy.

I let out a groan of frustration and mom puts her hand on my back. I look up from staring at the floor and see a nurse walk past the visiting room. As if this day isn't any less aggravating, I can't help but wish we knew more about Charlie. It's been a few hours since she's gotten out of surgery, but we can't go up and see her yet. Tony and Chris went in to sit with Riley for a bit which is good. He needs to get himself better so he can get out of that bed and up to see Charlie. I'm seriously going to beat the shit out of both of them for making us all sit here and worry like this.

My pocket starts to vibrate and I pull my phone out of my pocket. I read the text message I just got and a smile crosses my face. Fucking Emma and Pete are playing text message tag with me.

Emma – Let's go for a walk and grab some coffee....oh yeah and bring that cute brunette before Pete snags her ;)

After reading the message Emma and Pete walk over to me. I quickly tell mom that we're going down for some coffee and to call me if the doctors come back out here about Charlie.

I know what I need to do and I want to talk to her so bad. It's now or never and I can thank Emma and Pete for the push I've needed all day.

Walking across the visiting room I stop in front of Chloe. She looks up at me with those beautiful brown eyes and I ask her to come with us for a walk and coffee. Thank god she says yes and I pull her hand in mine.

And just like that the warmth she always brought when we were together spreads from my fingers to my hands and up my arm.

Chapter 24

CHLOE

Derrick lets go of my hand to grab both cups of coffee and walks over to the registers. I quickly pull out a twenty from my back pocket and hand it to the cashier. He gives me a handsome scowl and I just shrug my shoulders and give him a wink. I think it's a step in the right direction that we can still be so playful with one another after so many months apart.

Walking around the cafeteria to find a seat, I follow closely behind him. I watch as his body takes each step and I feel a sensation take over my body that I haven't felt in a long time. It's a feeling of longing. Seeing and being near him is bringing back so many emotions that I don't know what to do with. We need to talk, I should really tell him about the interview with the Red Sox on Monday, but I don't know where to start and how it will end. Will things be okay? Can we make this work? Will he even want to make it work?

We choose to sit down at a table by the window and I quickly grab the cup of coffee so that I have something to keep my hands busy. Playing with the cup I slide it back in forth between my hands waiting for it to cool down. My nerves are completely shot at this point and I don't know where to look or even what to say.

I take a sip of the steamy beverage and burn my lip.

"Ouch, shit that's hot!"

"Yeah I usually prefer my coffee hot. Don't you?" He says with a laugh.

"Yes smart ass I do. I just thought if I…you know what never mind." I say with a pout.

The moment turns into a minute of silence and then two minutes and before I know it ten minutes of awkward silence passes by and my coffee cup is empty.

"Ugh! Derrick, why does this feel so weird?" I ask motioning to the distance between us.

"It does doesn't it? Look I'm sorry for not calling you the past few months."

"Is there a reason you didn't call?" I ask staring out the window.

I don't know if I can make eye contact right now with him. As much as I wanted to call him so many times, I didn't.

"To tell you the truth, I don't know why I didn't call. At times I was pissed as hell with you and didn't think I could hear your voice, but then other times I just wanted to hear you so that I knew you weren't really gone."

I finally take my eyes off the view out the window and look at him. He really is the most handsome guy I've ever seen. Even though his blue eyes look tired and worn out, they still shine when he's looking at me. We can communicate so well with one another just by looking into the other's eyes.

"You know it's killed me every day not talking to you, regardless if I wanted to or not. I wake up thinking about you and how your day may go. I go to bed thinking about you and wonder if you would talk to me about how your day actually turned out. All day everyday I'm consumed thinking about you…thinking about us."

His words mean so much to me. He has no idea how much. I try to speak, but he asks me to wait.

"Chloe I know we said the distance was too much for us to handle this relationship, but to be honest I'd rather live thousands of miles away from you than not with you at all."

The smile on my face is so big that I'm afraid my face will split in two.

"Oh Derrick I feel the same way and I've missed you so much. I tried to forget about the pain of us being apart, to do things to help keep my mind from you, but nothing worked.

I don't know how to approach the topic of what I was really doing while we were apart, but I figure now isn't the time to bring up that kind of a conversation.

Derrick grabs the legs of my chair and pulls me closer to him.

"I need to touch you Chloe, it's been too long."

He's so close to me that I can feel his hot breathe on my face. I want so badly to close this space and feel those lips against mine. There's so much for us to talk about so many things that will change. But right now I just want to be close to him.

Grabbing my hands in his he brings them to his lips and peppers kisses along my knuckles and finger tips. My entire body is paralyzed with passion for this man and in that moment I swear to never let anything pull us apart again. I have to tell him…he needs to know.

DERRICK

Seeing Chloe today took my breath away. Nothing about her has changed. She is still as beautiful as the day I left her in LA. Her long dark hair still smells of her sweet mango shampoo and her gorgeous big, brown eyes still twinkle every time she smiles.

Sitting here with her and having her close to me is almost like a dream. For a brief moment I almost forgot why we were even here at Massachusetts General.

I need to touch her.

I need to make sure I'm not dreaming.

I need to know she isn't going to get up and walk away from me.

Pulling her chair closer to me I tell her that I need to touch her and I take her hands in mine. I look deep into her eyes and in that moment I felt it. Our souls found each other again and I know everything will be okay.

"Derrick I have to tell you something." She says.

I can only imagine. If it's the regret I know I have to talk to her about, I really don't want to hear about it. This moment is too perfect to spoil with the mistakes we've made while we were apart.

"Chloe it's not important, please I don't want to ruin this moment with you. I've been waiting for too long to be this close to you."

"But that's just it Derrick. You may never have to wait again."

As much as I want her to not talk, I'm intrigued with what she has to say. Maybe I was completely off and she isn't going to tell me about stuff from LA. I have to hear her out, so I nod and shut my mouth.

"Well since you left LA I pretty much drowned myself in work. I was lucky that my bosses Tom and Traci gave me the opportunity to work on the field for Super Bowl. Derrick it was the most amazing thing I've ever done in my entire life. In fact I liked it so much they kept putting me on for more work on the field to report games and interview the players and coaches."

The excitement she has beaming off of her is addicting, but I have no clue where this is all going.

"That's great Chloe. I'm so proud of you."

"Yeah and it gets better." She says.

She is so excited she's practically bouncing up and down in her seat and it's kind of turning me on. This is so wrong. My best friends are knocked out in this hospital and all I can think about is taking Chloe back to our home and fucking her senseless for hours…maybe even days.

"Derrick, you don't understand. Let me finish. So I kept working on the sidelines for a few games during the college basketball season and eventually got the chance to be on the court for most of March Madness this year. I was actually supposed to be there for the Final Four and the Championship game, but something else came up that was more important."

"Ah man Chloe, you know Charlie is going to hate that you missed out on that because you're here."

"No that's not it at all. I was never going to be there for the game anyway."

"I don't get it, where would you have been? March Madness would have been a huge opportunity for you."

"Actually a better opportunity did come up. You see I enjoyed being on the field for the football games and on the court for basketball, but really there's only one sport I feel connected to and that is baseball. Derrick, the Red Sox have a position for a Senior Analyst. The job is here in Boston and I wouldn't have to live across the country anymore. My final interview is here on April 8th when they play the Orioles."

I can't believe what Chloe is telling me. She has a chance to move back to Boston. My girl will be close enough that I can touch her, love her and be by her side every day.

Taking her face in my hands I can't hold back any longer. I look into her eyes and see the tears begin to fall to her cheeks. She nods her head to give me the go ahead and I kiss her like my life depends on it. The feel of our lips touching, our mouths connecting and the taste of Chloe is something I never want to miss again. We stay interlocked for what feels like forever when I hear a throat clear behind us.

We pull away and I can see that Pete and Emma are standing behind us with big smiles on their faces. I look over at my angel and I can see she has a smile on her face too.

"So did you guys talk or just make out the whole time?" Pete asks.

"Shut up asshole! Chloe just gave me some incredible news. She's coming back to Boston to work strictly with the Red Sox. She's going to be the Senior Analyst for the team. Isn't that incredible?"

"That's great Chloe, congrats." Emma says. "Does that mean I need to find a new place to live?"

"Oh god no Emma! You're always welcome at my…I mean our house. Right Chloe?"

I know I'm probably over stepping some toes on this one, but I can't kick out Emma. She's family and she needs that place to stay more that anyone, especially right now.

"You know what? This is all happening so fast. But Emma I'll say that if Derrick wants you to stay then you stay. I really haven't even considered where I would be living."

"What are you talking about Angel? You'll live in our house." I tell her with all sincerity. I don't think she understands how much all of this means to me right now.

"Okay Derrick let's just step back for a second okay. I still need to get through my final interview and then move all my shit back home. Let's take it one day at a time, okay?"

"Whatever you say Angel, you just made me the happiest guy in all of Boston. I have my girl with me and knowing that you could be coming back home is enough for me. At least for right now."

"Fair enough." She says and kisses me on the lips.

"Well if you two lovebirds can keep it in your pants for a few more hours, why don't we go up and check on Char and Riley?" Pete says.

"Yeah by now we should be good to go up and see Charlie."

Pete and Emma start to walk away and as Chloe begins to stand I grab her in my arms.

"Thank you." I tell her.

"For what?" She whispers.

"For never forgetting how this feels." I tell her as I guide my touch along her cheek, her arm and across her back until both my arms are wrapped around her body.

This is where I want to be. This is what makes me feel safe. This is where I know my love needs to stay.

Chapter 25

CHLOE

Derrick takes my hand in his and guides me out of the cafeteria and into the hallway. I watch as his tall, strong form leads me in the right direction. He makes me smile and my heart does flip flops. Derrick has always been so sure about everything in our relationship and I let him down. But this time I'm never going to lose sight of what he means to me....he is my world.

I feel like a kid again. It's difficult to explain the emotions running through my mind. For the past few months I've been trying to let go of something that never should have been missing from my life. I made a choice and thankfully it was a decision that didn't ruin what I have right here.

Squeezing his hand a little tighter, he starts to rub his thumb along my knuckles. It feels so good to have his touch provide warmth through my body.

There's a lot we need to talk about and I'm sure the time will come. I just don't know how I'll approach what happened with Andrew and me. Lying and hiding it from Derrick is not an option, we will not go back into a relationship telling lies. Once things are more certain with Char's health, I'll sit him down and tell him everything...I mean everything.

I follow Emma, Pete and Derrick into the elevator. Just a little over an hour ago we were on this same elevator and I was worried about how I could even look Derrick in the eye. Now we're heading back up to our families like we never were apart. My heart skips a beat at the thought of being with Derrick again. I know I've missed him. I've felt the loss of his love in my life and now that he's here, right next to me, I believe that everything will be okay.

We stand in the elevator moving up toward the fourth floor and Derrick wraps his arms around my waist pulling me in closer to him. I feel his body up against my back and can smell his scent with how close we're standing. I close my eyes for a brief moment to take it all in. All of this feels like a dream. Char and Riley's accident, being here with Derrick, it all brings out so many emotions I don't know what to do with.

The elevator stops on the floor and we all exit walking toward the visiting room. Derrick grabs onto my hand and holds on for dear life. I'm sure he feels my hesitation walking in like this with both our parents sitting in there, but to be honest, I don't really care. Mom and dad love Derrick and I know that Rose and Bud will be happy to know we've worked through our issues.

The thing is we really haven't. In just under an hour I have rekindled my relationship with Derrick and according to him, I'll be moving back in as soon as I fly back to Boston. Hell, I wouldn't put it past him to hire someone to go out there and move me back so I don't have to return to LA.

As we walk in the room all eyes are on me and Derrick. With our hands still interlocked, Derrick raises them in the air. He's a complete nut and I love him for it. Rose and mom both get up and walk on over and pull us into a giant group hug. A smile creeps across my face and it feels so good to be with our families like this. I hate the reason that we were brought here today, but at the same time it's because of this accident that Derrick and I had to come to terms with our true feeling for each other.

Now we just need for Char to wake up so that the day is perfect.

We pull away from our moms and both of them have tears running down their faces.

"I don't know what happened on that walk you four took, but I'm happy to see this." Mom says grabbing onto our hands.

"I agree."Rose says. "You two belong together. No distance should stop you from loving one another."

Derrick looks over at me and gives me the look. I know what he thinks I should do and I don't know if I should tell them yet. What if I don't get the job?

He sees the reluctance in my eyes and pulls me into him bringing his arm around my shoulders.

"Chloe just shared some great news with me that I think you all will want to hear. Isn't that right angel?"

I give him the look of death and pull myself from his embrace.

"Well I really didn't want to say anything till I knew for sure, but since someone has a big mouth I guess I need to tell you." I look at Derrick again with daggers coming from my eyes.

He smiles at me, his baby blue eyes filled with happiness and kisses me on the forehead.

"Go ahead tell them. We can all use some good news today."

I take in a deep breath and let it all out. I know everyone will be happy about this news. It's just that I wasn't ready to share it with everyone till I knew for sure.

"So long story short, after I worked the Super Bowl, I was asked to look into a position as a field analyst."

Everyone is now up on their feet, including dad and Bud, waiting for me to say what they all know is going to come out of my mouth.

I look around the room at the seven people staring back at me.

"The Red Sox have been interviewing me for the past few weeks for a permanent position with the team. Monday is my final interview when they play the Orioles. If they like what I do, the job will be mine. I'll be coming back home for good."

The entire room lets out a silent cheer and I'm once again pulled into a giant hug.

It feels so good to know they all want me here, back home, where I belong.

DERRICK

The past few months have sucked, they've really sucked, but now it's like they never happened. I had hoped that Chloe and I would find our way back together, but this…this is just a dream come true. Having Chloe here, standing next to me, is better than I could have ever dreamed.

It's not the ideal moment for us to reunite, but at this point I'll take what I can get. I stand back and watch as our families hug her like their lives depend on it. Even though I know she didn't want to tell them yet, I still wanted her to give them something to look forward to.

When I saw our moms' eyes light up at us holding hands when we walked into the room, I knew they needed a little bit more to make them smile.

Her telling them she is coming home did just that.

Everyone begins to pull away from the group hug and I take my girl's hand back in mine.

"Hey do you want to go to see Riley with me? I think he could use some of your badass humor and banter the two of you got going on together."

"Is that really why you want me to go in there with you? Or do you just want to tell him the news that I may be coming back to Boston?"

Chloe looks at me with those deep, dark brown eyes and I know she can see straight to my soul. There's no use lying to her because she'll know the truth as soon as we walk into his room.

"Okay you got me. But can you really blame me. I want to tell everyone that you're mine again. I don't know when I have felt this good Chloe. The past four months have been a living hell and now I feel like I have a reason, a purpose to get up in the morning. You have no idea how happy you've made me today angel."

She turns her body to completely face me and takes my face into her small hands. Looking me straight in the eye I know she is about to cry.

"Derrick the day I walked away from you at the airport was one of the worst days of my life. I'm so happy that I'm here with you and that you're giving me another chance to show you how happy we can be together. I still love you Derrick. I never stopped. This is all just a lot to take in with Char and us together again. I think I'm just a bit overwhelmed."

"I know and I'm sorry if I'm being a bit pushy, it's just that I've missed everything about you and don't want to waste another second…"

"Hold that thought Derrick. Let's get in to see Riley before we get too involved. Okay?"

"Good thinking, let's go."

I kiss her forehead and interlace our fingers together. Walking past Emma, we let her know we're going back to see Riley and to come get us if there's any news on Char.

Chloe and I walk side by side down the hallway and through the doors leading to Riley's room. When we get to his door it's closed and I can hear the nurse through the other side giving him instructions. We wait a few moments and in no time Riley and the nurse are coming out of the room.

"What's this, they're letting you free already?" I ask both him and the nurse.

"Yeah, all I have are a few broken bones and a few scraps." He nods his head toward Chloe. "Hey girl thanks for flying all the way out here to see me. Don't you think Char will get a little jealous?"

Chloe smacks the arm, not in a cast, and reaches her arms around him in a hug.

"So now what?" I ask looking directly at the nurse.

"Mr. Kincaid is right. The doctors put a cast on him to help set his collar bone in place. The rest will just have to heal in time. All of the other tests show that he's fine to be released today, but I did warn him to take it easy, get some rest and use the pain meds if he gets too uncomfortable."

"No worries, Nurse Nancy, I'll be a good boy." Riley says winking at the nurse.

"Well since you're free to go let's go back out and see what we can find out about Char." Chloe says taking my hand back in hers.

"So no word yet?" Riley asks.

"No and we're all getting pretty antsy about not knowing what is going on, it's been long enough by now. We should be able to get into see her soon." I say.

When we walk out into the visitor room, both Bryce and Teresa are standing in the corner talking to the doctor. Hopefully he has some good news to tell us because this waiting shit sucks.

Chloe and I sit down next to mom and Emma, while Riley makes his way over to Bryce and Teresa.

I can see that Bryce is trying to comfort Teresa by running his hand up and down her back. She is glued to his side and as soon as Riley walks over she swings an arm around his waist.

After a few minutes the doctor pats Bryce on the back and walks out of the room. The three of them walk over to us and have a seat in the row of chairs directly across from where we're sitting.

"Will someone please say something?" Chloe says.

"Of course, honey. I think I'm just in a bit of shock." Teresa says holding onto Bryce with one arm and Riley with the other.

Fucking hell woman just spit it out already. I'm growing more and more impatient the longer these three keep looking at one another.

And then Riley speaks up to break the silence.

"Well she won't be coming home anytime soon, but they are happy with her progress. She has responded to a lot of the tests they've been doing on her which is good and shows normal brain activity. They also just took her off the respirator and she is breathing on her own again."

Riley stops talking and runs his fingers through his hair. "Why the fuck didn't you tell me she was this bad?" He looks between me and Emma.

"Riley we couldn't have you going crazy while you were under care too. Don't be mad at us now. You're up to date now and know that she'll be fine." Emma says.

"That's my girl up there. I would have liked to know what was happening. God what if something worse would have happened? I wouldn't have been able to live with myself."

Riley gets up and shoves his hand in his pocket and begins to pace behind the row of chairs. I see him pull out a box and I know exactly what he's holding. I look over at Chloe while she watches him.

"Riley what is that in your hand?" She asks.

He looks up at her with tears in his eyes.

"It's the ring I'm going to give my future wife when she gets out of that bed." He says. "Teresa, Bryce I'm going up to see her. I can't wait any longer to see my girl."

And with that Riley sticks the box back in his pocket and walks out the room. I can't even begin to feel what he is going through right now. I would kill anyone to take away Chloe's pain if we were in this situation.

I just thank god that Char is progressing.

Now she just needs to wake the fuck up.

Chapter 26

CHLOE

Watching Riley walk away after seeing him hold that ring is tearing at my heart strings. Char is an amazing woman and I'm so happy that she's found her one true love. After all she went through during her relationship with Marc, I'm glad she has a guy like Riley to make her happy.

Mom and dad walk over to us and sit down in their seats. Derrick still has my hand in his and he's rubbing circles along the backside of my hand. I want to break the unnerving silence that is growing between us, but I don't know what to say. I look around the room and see that everyone is pretty much staring off into space.

Chris and Tony get up and walk over to Pete. They've been here ever since they brought me and I'm sure they want to get home to their families.

I decide to sit back further in my chair and rest my head on Derrick's shoulders. The comfort of him here with me makes me feel at ease and my eyelids begin to droop till they close. I feel a warm hand touching my face and recognize the caress as something Derrick would do to help me fall asleep or relax.

I must have dozed off for a bit and when I wake up I see that the room has emptied quite a bit. In fact the only people in the room are me, Derrick and a few other people I don't know.

"Hey sleepy, how are you feeling?" Derrick asks brushing a few stray pieces of hair from my eyes.

"I guess I was a more tired than I thought. Sorry for passing out like that. Where is everyone?" I ask.

"Your parents went up to see Char and everyone else went home." He replies.

"Can we go up to see her?"

"Of course, let's go."

Derrick stands first and grabs both of my hands to help me up. We walk hand in hand to the elevator and he doesn't let go. Since Char is in the ICU unit, we all can't go in at the same time to see her. When we get up to her floor Mom and Dad are sitting in the visitor's room and smile as soon as we walk in.

"How is she? Did you get to go in and see her yet?" I ask sitting next to mom.

She nods her head and a smile crosses her face. "We were just in to see her and she's still asleep. She looks so peaceful lying there. I didn't want to stay too long since Riley wanted to be with her. I'm afraid that boy won't leave her side till she wakes up."

"I'd really like to go in and see her Mom."

"You can, it's okay if she has two visitors at a time. Dad and I are going to go home and get some rest, but will be back first thing tomorrow morning. I suggest after you sit with her for a bit you do the same."

"I know, I will. I'm pretty tired from the flight but the nap I just took sure helped me feel a little better."

"Good, I'm glad sweetie. Do you want us to leave the door open or will you be going back to your house with Derrick?"

I look between the three of them, my mom, dad and Derrick. They all seem to assume I'll be staying with Derrick and have smiles on all their faces.

"Geez guys, I can only assume you want me to stay with Derrick and I surely won't argue. You can lock up tonight. I think I'll be fine."

"Okay honey, we're going to go, but call us if you need anything."

I stand with my parents and give them both a big hug whispering into my mom's ear that I'll be fine and that I love her so much.

Derrick and I walk them to the elevator and then into the hallway leading to Char's room.

"I'll be right out here when you're ready to go. Take your time, no rush."

He pulls me into his warm body and holds onto me tightly. The feel of him against me is overwhelming. I've missed his touch too much. We pull apart and he kisses me on the lips. I can taste his minty breath and for a brief moment I'm absorbed into him and only him.

I blink a few times and pull myself out of my la-la-land remembering that I'm about to go in and see my sister.

"I won't be too long. Then we can go home and spend some time together."

"Sounds good angel, I can't wait." He says and lets go of my hand.

I walk through the two tall doors and down the hallway. I can see the top of Riley's head and make my way to her room. He's sitting up against her bed and has her left hand in his. His head is down and he doesn't see that I'm in the room.

"Hey Riley." I whisper. "I didn't want to scare you, but is it okay that I sit with her for awhile?"

He gets up from his seat and pulls me into a hug. Riley and I have only met a few times, but we seem to have found an instant connection to one another. He's a good guy and the best fit for my little sister. He makes her happy and that in turn makes me even happier. I don't mind him marrying her, even if it means I have to deal with his sarcasm for the rest of my life.

"I'm going to go get some water, be good to my girl while I'm away." He looks down into my eyes and I can see that his are filled with tears. "She'll come back to us soon, she just needs her rest and when she's ready those amazing eyes will open again."

Riley moves behind me and exits Char's room closing the door behind him.

I look back over at my baby sister. We're only a few years apart, yet she'll always be my little sister. She looks so small lying there in the hospital bed. Her long dark hair is pulled up and some is matted to her forehead from the gauze. Her face looks pale, which for her is different since she has an amazing complexion.

Sitting down in Riley's seat, I take Char's hand in mine. I look at her hand, her nails and then back up at her face. Tears begin to fall from my eyes and onto the blue blanket covering her body.

"Oh Char! I'm so sorry you're lying in this bed. If there's any way I could change places with you I would, I swear I would. This whole thing shouldn't have happened to you and Riley. Today, well I assume, was going to be a special day for you guys…and it got shot to hell. I'm sorry for being a lousy big sister. I'm sorry for moving away from you and Derrick. I screwed up Char, I screwed up big time. I'm grateful that he wants to take me back. Yeah can you believe it…me either? He's such a great guy and I'm so lucky to have both of you in my life. I need you to wake up Char, if you can hear me wake up. I need you Char. I need to have some girl time with you and need to talk to you about some stuff. Damn it Char please wake up. I need you…we all need you."

I get up from the chair and walk around the room. I need to get this off my chest. Derrick is the one that should hear what an awful person I really am, but not just yet, not right now. I look over at Char's sleeping form and wish I'd have done things differently. If I would have just kept to myself and stayed away from him, I wouldn't feel this guilt.

I just hope when they know, they won't all hate me.

DERRICK

The visitor's room outside the ICU has completely cleared out and for right now I have some peace and quiet. Today has been the day from hell and it seems to be lasting forever. As happy as I am that Chloe is home and back in my life, I'm still feeling uneasy about Charlie in the hospital.

She's a tough cookie and I know she'll pull through this. I just wish it wasn't her that had to be in that room. Of all people Charlie is the most selfless, caring and compassionate person I know. She deserves to be enjoying her engagement to Riley right now, not knocked out in a hospital room.

I see Riley walk out the doors and look over in his direction. His arm is in a huge cast and he looks like he could use a break. He walks over in my direction and has a seat right next to me.

"This sucks man." He says running his hand through his hair.

"I know pal, but she'll be okay. This is Charlie we're talking about. She's too stubborn to let a little head injury get her down. Plus if she knew we were worrying about her she'd kick our asses."

"She's going to be okay Derrick. She has to be, I can't live without her." He says with a look of panic across his face.

"No worries Riley. She'll be good as new in no time."

"Yeah I guess. The doctors and nurses keep saying her vitals and other activity are impressive considering her injury. I just want her to open her eyes. She means the world to me and I hate that there's nothing I can do to help her right now."

I can't even begin to imagine what he feels like right now. The love of his life is lying helpless in a hospital bed and there's nothing any of us can do to wake her up.

"Ya know she needs her rest and when she's good and ready she'll get up. Charlie is miserable if you wake her before she's ready, so let's just give her some time. Why don't you go home and get some rest. I'm sure the nurses will call if anything changes. You need to be awake and alert when she comes out of this."

"No way in hell Derrick. You can't ask me to leave her side for that long. What if she wakes up and I'm not there. She needs to see me when she wakes up." He says getting up and starts pacing the room.

"Okay man I get it. Chloe and I are going to go back to the house when she gets out. You want me to bring you anything back."

"So I guess you two are okay now?"

"I don't know what you mean by okay, but I'm going to do whatever I need to do so that we can be happy again. I think we have a lot to talk about. I can guarantee she'll get the job with the Red Sox and soon after I'll have her moved back in to our house."

"You're going to tell her about you and Trisha, right?"

"Hell man, like I don't know I have to do that bad enough. If I'd have known Chloe and I had any chance at getting back together. I never would have went over to her house. I'll tell Chloe when we talk, but I hope to fuck it doesn't' change things between us. It would fucking break me if it ruined our chances to be together again, it would destroy me Riley."

"Yeah, I get than man, but you have to come clean…both of you. I'm sure she's got some secrets to share too. Regardless of what you two did you have to know before going into things again. It'll only get worse if she finds out later."

"Alright, I hear you. She's going to come back to my place tonight and we'll talk, but believe me talking with her is the last thing I want to do. I've missed her for months Riley. This is going to fucking suck."

"No more than my life sucks right now." He says sitting back down next to me.

Riley's words hit home hard and I hate that I'm complaining about my issues when Charlie is knocked out.

"I'm sorry man that was wrong of me."

"Nah, no worries Derrick. I know it sucks for both of us."

Chloe comes walking out of the double doors and into the visitor's room. I watch as she walks over to us with tear stained cheeks and a wad of tissues in her hand. Pulling her into my lap she lets out a sob and I do my best to comfort her.

Riley pats me on the back and gets up from his seat.

"I'm going back in to sit with her. Bring me back some clean clothes when you guys come back tomorrow."

"You got it. Let me know if you need anything else."

He nods his head and walks out of the room and back to his girl.

I rub my hand up Chloe's back and grab her chin in my fingers. "Hey angel. She's going to be okay. Let's get home and rest. We'll come back tomorrow."

I help Chloe get to her feet and hold her by my side the entire way to the car. The entire ride to our house is silent and I'm growing nervous the closer we get. I know that we both agreed on our breakup and in reality I didn't do anything wrong, but the guilt I feel is really starting to eat at me.

"Do you want me to get you something to eat before we get home?" I ask to break the silence.

"No thanks. I really just want to get into bed and sleep." She says laying her head against my shoulder.

"Okay angel, then we'll get you home showered and in bed."

She nods her head and I continue on our way home.

No matter how much it's going to suck to have this conversation, we need to do it. And I'm willing to do just about anything to keep Chloe as my girl.

Chapter 27

CHLOE

The silence between us is driving me nuts and the closer we get to his house, I mean our house the sooner I'll have to tell him everything. My stomach is tied up in knots. Derrick asks me if I want anything to eat and I start to feel the bile creep up my throat. I've never felt like this before. The guilt of what happened between Andrew and I is eating me alive and the fear of not knowing how Derrick will react is even worse.

I know that Derrick and I were broken up, but it doesn't stop the feeling that I did something wrong. What I did was wrong…right?

God this is going to kill me. The sooner I come clean and tell him the faster I'll know his reaction. If this destroys my chances to be with him again, I'll never forgive myself. The anxiety of not knowing how he'll react is killing me. I just want to spit it out and get it over with.

We pull into the driveway and a million memories come flooding back into my mind. Derrick takes my hand and pulls it to his lips, he places a gentle kiss to each of my knuckles and stares into my eyes.

"Come on angel, we're home. I can't wait for you to see some of the things I did inside. Everything we wanted to do has been a work in progress, but I know you'll like the changes."

I smile at his excitement and tell him I know I'll love it.

He gets out of the car and tells me to wait. Being the gentleman he is he comes around to my side and opens the door.

"Oh shit!" I shout.

"What? What's wrong?" Derrick asks with a confused look on his face.

"My bags. I left them in Pete's truck."

A smirk crosses Derrick's face as he walks to the back of his car and pops the trunk.

"Nope, I have them right here." He says pulling them out and dragging them up the driveway.

I just shake my head and follow him up to our front porch. He pulls out his keys and unlocks the door walking into our home.

"Emma is going to stay over at Riley and Char's tonight to keep an eye on Manny."

"Okay."

"So….are you sure you don't want to eat anything?' He asks putting my bags by the stairs.

I walk around and take in everything Derrick has done to upgrade our home. In just a few short months he's done so much and I love it all. I walk back out to where he's standing with his hands on his hips looking damn proud of himself...for good reason.

From head to toe Derrick is an incredibly good looking man. I've really taken him for granted throughout the past few years and I know now more than ever how important he is to me. I walk over to him and he stretches his arms out to me. I walk into his embrace and lean my body tightly up against his.

"Chloe, please tell me I'm not dreaming all of this."

I let out a giggle.

"No Derrick you're not dreaming. I'm here, in our home and in your arms. It's exactly where I want to be."

"Exactly where you should be angel."

We stay linked together for a few minutes and then begin to part. I look up into his baby blues and want so badly to kiss him, to touch him and to make love to him. But first we need to talk and I'm so afraid it will change everything. I don't want it to ruin this moment, yet I can't wait another second.

"Derrick, we need to talk."

I turn my body from his and walk toward our living room. Sitting down on the soft couch, I pat the cushion next to me indicating that I want him to sit down.

"Chloe, I know we need to talk. I have some things I need to tell you too, it's just…."

I stop him. He can't be the first to tell me what he has to say. I have to do this, no matter what happens…he has to know.

"No Derrick please let me go first."

He nods his head and sits down next to me.

"I want you to know that I'm so happy to be here with you right now. There's nowhere in the world I'd rather be than in your arms. I just need to let you know about something that happened while we were apart."

Derrick is staring intently into my eyes and a huge lump begins to form in my throat. My hands are sweating and my knees are shaking. I feel like I'm about to have an out of body experience in my own god damn living room.

"Relax, okay Chloe. We were apart and neither one of us knew we'd be back here together. If you don't think you can talk about it yet we can wait."

I shake my head. "No, I want you to know everything. It's the only way I'll feel right moving on with us. I don't want to feel guilt like this again. It's tearing me up inside."

"I know, I feel the same way. So let's just get everything out and see how we feel about it…okay."

He runs his hand down along the side of my face and I lean into him. How did I ever get lucky enough to have this man in my life?

"I stayed to myself for the most part, but then I just couldn't sulk anymore. A good friend and my co-analyst Trent urged me to go out with the crew a few times."

I look up at him and he nods his head encouraging me to continue.

"Well then I started working closely with a certain sport's figure and after tapings he'd come out to the club with us. I pushed him off for quite awhile and then I let all my walls crumble."

I put my head in my hands and begin to cry. "I'm so sorry Derrick. I'm so sorry."

DERRICK

I hate to see her cry, but I know that she needs to release the guilt she feels. Shit the guilt we both feel.

This is fucking crazy, neither one of use should feel guilty. We both walked away from each other that day at the airport. Who knew we'd be together like this again?

In my heart I knew she'd always be the one, but to be together like this…I didn't think it would ever happen again.

I have a good idea I know exactly who the certain sport's guy she's referring to and it pisses me off to know he had his hands on my girl. I want to comfort her, but at the same time it kills me that she let those walls down to another man. I really don't even know that I care to know how far she let him go, but I have a feeling she needs to tell me.

We sit here in silence on the couch we bought together, in the living room that holds so many memories of us in, and in the house that we bought to be our home. There are no words to really describe the pain we've gone through and the hurt we may have to bare while we continue our talk.

Right now, I know I'm the emotionally stronger person out of the two of us, so I just come out and ask.

"Did you sleep with him?"

She pulls her head from hands and looks me in the eye. I don't know if I'll like the response I'm about to hear, but I have to be prepared for just about anything.

"No, I didn't sleep with him. I didn't let it get that far…I couldn't. But I'm still a bad person Derrick. I let him see a side of me that I only ever showed you. We may not have been intimate, but we did things that I regret."

My blood is beginning to boil and I really don't give a fuck about the details. As much as I love this woman I need to move past what she's done…what I've done. I can live with the fact that she didn't sleep with him. Because if she did it would be so much worse, it would break my heart.

"Look, I'm not happy you let another man touch what's mine. I hate the fact that he saw you in a way that only my eyes were ever meant to see. But I love you more than life itself Chloe and we'll work through this. I wasn't a saint while we were apart either. In fact I sat around and drove Emma, Charlie and Derrick nuts when I wasn't out with Pete, but I too let my guard down and found myself in a situation I now regret."

"Did you sleep with her?" Chloe asks in a whisper.

"Hell no!" I shout making her jump.

I grab her up in my arms and look her in those amazing dark eyes.

"Sorry. No I didn't. I left before we could get any further than a kiss." I tell her trying to maintain eye contact so she knows how awful this makes me feel.

She turns her head away and leaves out a heavy sigh. She slowly turns back in my direction. She looks at me, tears streaming down her beautiful face.

"We have a history Chloe. We have something that not many people can say that they've ever experienced. I know that what I did with the other woman was nothing, I mean it meant nothing. I don't want to dwell on the past. Instead I want to work on our future. You're my future Chloe. No one can ever take your place in my heart…ever."

"Are you sure you can get past the time we were apart? I know you say it now that we can just move past it, but I want to make sure. I don't want us moving forward again to only have to step back."

"Chloe I can tell you that I fucking hated every second we were apart. I tried for a long time to figure out how we could get back together and make the distance work. No matter how much I wanted to call you, I just couldn't. I wanted you to come to me."

"Derrick I'll never make the same mistake twice. There's no turning back now. You're it for me and no matter what happens you are my home."

She slides onto my lap and kisses me hard. I'm instantly consumed with her and want nothing more than to take her up to our bed and make love to her all night long.

"I've missed you so much angel, let me take you to bed and show you." I tell her kissing her again on the lips.

"Yes please Derrick, I want to be with you so badly. You have no idea how much I've missed your touch."

I lift her up off my lap and we make our way up the stairs and into our bedroom.

Today has been one hell of a day, but I promise to make it one memorable night.

As we walk into the room, she immediately takes in the changes I've made. I watch as she walks toward the bathroom and I know exactly what she's looking for. She enters the bathroom, flips the light and turns and smiles as I follow close behind.

"It's beautiful Derrick. This is exactly the tub I wanted. It's perfect."

"Well I never thought of a bathroom as beautiful, but now that you're standing in it I can agree."

We bring our bodies together and as we begin to kiss we slowly start to undress one another. I want to take my time touching every inch of her tonight. I move toward the shower and turn on the water.

"Thank you for loving me Derrick. I promise to love you every day for the rest of my life and never take you for granted again."

"You never have to thank me Chloe. I was made to love you."

While we shower under the warm water we kiss and touch every part of one another. As much as I've missed her the past few months, I didn't realize how starved for her I really was until tonight.

Once we're both clean from head to toe we exit the shower and move out into the bedroom.

I watch as she lets the towel drop to the floor and move slowly into our bed. Her body is fucking amazing. I can't wait to get inside of her and feel her warmth.

Climbing up the bed, I kiss her legs, her stomach, her tits and finally land on her lips. Our tongues immediately find one another and the taste of her is intoxicating. I can't get enough.

"Derrick, please…don't make me wait any longer. I need you inside me. Now."

I don't speak. I don't ask any questions. I do exactly as she says.

Leaning over her body I push myself into her wet pussy and immediately we find our rhythm. I pump my cock in and out while I kiss her mouth, her neck and lick trails of my tongue along her collar bone.

The sweet sounds of her moans tell me I'm giving her exactly what she wants. But I know at this pace there's no way I'll last long.

"Derrick, I'm close. Come with me."

"I'm already there angel."

I can feel her tight pussy cling onto me as I continue to ride into her until I find my release.

This has been an incredible night being with her and I'm so thankful she's here with me right now. Being with her like this is exactly where we I'm supposed to be. Chloe is mine and I'll make her happy for the rest of her life. .

I don't care if she gets the fucking job with the Red Sox or not. She's coming home to me and we will never be a part again. Chloe has been my girl for years. She's the reason I've wanted to be a better man. And she is the one that will make my life complete.

Chapter 28

CHLOE

I wake feeling warm because I'm wrapped in his arms. I've missed this feeling and I'm not too sure if this is a dream. When I open my eyes it will take me back to reality, to the day to day life I have back in Los Angeles that Derrick is no longer a part of.
Suddenly my eyes go wide open. I look around the room, our room. I'm in our home in Boston and my heart begins to flutter. I'm exactly where I want to be and I couldn't be happier.

After the long day of flying into Boston and sitting at the hospital we came home and had the talk I've been dreading since we reconnected. I'm not proud of the things I've done in my life. I seem to never look out for others. I make life all about me…just Chloe. I really am not a good person to the people that care about me the most, but not anymore.

Coming back here yesterday made me realize that this really is my home. This is where I'm supposed to build my life. As much as I hate the time I've spent away from my family, I can't say I regret the opportunity to live on my own. I believe that because of my choice to move away, I gained a better appreciation for what I really have here.

I'm the luckiest girl in the world to have a man like Derrick to care for me and want to start a future. I cannot and will not take him for granted ever again.

Today is a new start for me.

I want to make sure that everyone that loves me knows that I would do anything for them.

I can guarantee some people, including myself, will be taken back by my sudden change in my ways. It's important to be there for the people you care about and not just a shallow person that only looks out for her.

There's a lot of stuff to take care of starting with reaching out to Trent and Andrew.

Trent was my best friend while living in LA. He did his best to make sure I was taking care of myself and I want him to know how much I really appreciate all that he's done for me. I want him to know that he's always welcome to come and visit us in Boston and that I'll still be there for him even if we're miles away from each other.

As for Andrew I owe him an apology for leading him on that night, if that is what really happened. Even if I was drinking a bit more than usual he deserves to know that my heart is with another man. What we did was a huge mistake and it's only fair if he knows the truth.

I want to turn over a new way of life and by starting with these two men I can begin to work toward the closure I need to move past my life in LA.

Tomorrow is my chance to start my new career here. Getting the field analyst position with the Red Sox would be a dream come true. Not only will I be able to work side by side with my favorite team, but I'll also be able to stay close to my family and Derrick.

I feel like things are starting to work out just the way I need them to. For once I'm going to put my loved ones first. It's time to take care of them instead of them always watching out for me.

Pulling myself from Derrick's arms I make my way to the bathroom to freshen up. I brush my teeth, pull my hair back in a pony tail and wash my face. I feel much more awake now and want to make Derrick breakfast before we go back to the hospital to see Char.

Once out in the kitchen I start rooting through the refrigerator and pantry. Thankfully Emma and Derrick are keeping the house stocked with food. I grab out the eggs, peppers, onions and ham. Derrick loves his western omelets so this will be the perfect food to make him breakfast in bed. I start up the Keurig once the pan is full of the omelet and brew us both a mug of coffee. I grab out the breakfast tray from the pantry and put the plate, napkin and fork in the center. I carefully carry everything up stairs without dropping it or spilling a drop of coffee. Kicking the door slightly with my foot, it swings open and I see Derrick start to stir in bed. I set the tray on my side and crawl in next to him.

His back is to me so I start running my nails lightly up and down his back. He starts to twitch and before he goes crazy from his tickle spots I kiss him on the back of his neck and wrap my arms around his chest.

"Hey Derrick, I made you breakfast in bed. Come on sleepy time to wake up." I say in a whisper.

He rolls over on his side and pulls me into his chest. I can hear his heart beat and a smile immediately crosses my face. This man's heart beats strong for me, for him….for us.

"I don't know that I've slept that good in months. It was so good to have you here next to me angel." He says and kisses my forehead.

"I couldn't agree more." I respond pulling myself in closer to his body.

"Good, so when can I have all your stuff moved back in to our home?" He asks in a whisper.

"We can make the arrangement tomorrow." I reply.

Derrick flips over in the bed so fast I almost fall off the side. He quickly grabs my body and slides me underneath him. I can feel his growing erection through my shorts and my panties become wetter by the minute. He kisses my neck and trails his tongue along my jaw line bringing his lips to mine. He kisses me passionately and I let out a moan.

"Chloe you just made me very happy. I never want to be apart from you again. Are you sure this is what you want?"

He takes in a quick breath from his sudden ramble of words and starts kissing me again. His tongue sweeps into my mouth and I get lost in the feel of Derrick. He spreads my legs apart with his knees and pushes himself in closer to my aching core.

I've missed his touch so badly over the past few months I just want him inside of me.

We continue to kiss like we're taking our last breathes.

He pulls away and looks me in the eye. Without words I know his soul is communicating with mine. It's so good to be this close to him again and I swear I'll never let him go.

We make love in our bed, in our home and for the first time in awhile I feel like I'm giving myself to someone else. It's time I do things right for this man right here. He deserves to be happy and I'll do just that for the rest of my life.

DERRICK

This morning was amazing.

I woke up to Chloe running her hands up and down my back and then was given the best surprise…she's really going to move back to Boston, like now.

Shit, if this is a dream, please don't wake me up.

Not only did she share that fucktasitic news with me, but she also made me my favorite omelet for breakfast. Too bad it was ice cold by the time I got to eat it, but we did use the time wisely to get reacquainted with one another a few times.

After we finally got untangled from the sheets, Chloe and I fed each other breakfast and then took a quick shower. Well it was meant to be a quick shower.

On our way over to the hospital all I can think about is our conversation after breakfast this morning. Something seems to be different with Chloe, but I can't quite put my finger on it. I was totally thrown off by her comment about calling to have her things moved so quickly. I thought for sure that I would have an argument on my hands with her on that one, but she really wants to come back home. I'm so happy about the whole situation. I really don't want to ask questions. All I care about is that Chloe is here with me now and she'll be moving into our home again to stay.

I look over at her as I drive down the highway. Chloe looks absolutely perfect and she is my whole world. Her long dark hair is lying along her shoulder in waves and I hate that I can't see her eyes with her giant sunglasses hiding her face. I look down along her body and she is wearing the cutest sundress and sweater. She is the most beautiful thing I've ever seen and she is all mine.

The conversation we had last night could have ruined any chance of us getting back together, but when it really comes down to it we love one another. Chloe and I have been through too much to allow anything destroy what we had and what we still have.

We pull into the parking deck and I hear Chloe let out a deep breath.

"You okay angel?"

"Hmm, what did you say?" She asks.

"I asked if you were okay."

"Yeah, sorry. I guess I'm just a little nervous. Now that we know Char has no serious damage to her organs or brain I just wish she would wake up. I know it's silly but I really want to be there for her. When she wakes up I want to be the sister she needs, not the one she has to take of anymore. I've got a lot of making up to do to her and I want to start as soon as those big brown eyes open up."

"I think that's great Chloe and Charlie will be so happy to know that you'll be back here in Boston for good. You'll see everything is going to turn out just as it always should have been. I can't wait to have you home with me every morning and every night again. You have no idea how much I've missed you being close enough to touch."

"I know Derrick, me too. I promise to make things right this time. Tomorrow I'll get the job and move everything back home. We can start from scratch and build up from there."

I shake my head and swallow hard the lump that is now in my throat.

"Chloe, I don't want to start over with you. We have years of love, passion and a connection that is impossible to forget. Yes, we were apart for four fucking long as hell months. But now we just move past that hurdle and pick up where we left off. I'm willing to make it work and try whatever we need to be together, are you?"

"Of course I am. I wasn't kidding when I said I wanted to move back home. This is where I need to be, where I want to be and there's no one else I would ever want to have a future with other than you Derrick. This is it for me. I promise you…we are my forever."

"Good. That's my girl. Now let's go in and see how Charlie is holding up and give Riley some clean clothes."

As soon as we get out of the car, Chloe comes to my side and holds onto my hand. I'm loving the instant connection she is determined to share and I can't help the giant smile that is spread across my face.

This morning the visitor's room is much fuller than it was yesterday and I immediately see Bryce and Teresa sitting in the far end of the room. Chloe and I walk over to them and they greet us both with a hug.

"How were things last night?" I hear Teresa ask.

"Things are great. Right Derrick?" She asks looking at me and squeezing my hand.

"You got that right angel, things are damn near perfect."

"Any word on how Char is doing?" Chloe asks looking between both of her parents.

"The doctor said she is doing remarkably well. Her vitals are normal, her brain activity is great and the swelling is almost completely down. She just needs to wake up." Bryce says.

"Well I'm going to go in and visit for a bit, give Riley a break." Chloe says letting go of my hand and giving me a kiss on the lips.

I watch as she walks away through the double doors leading to Charlie. My heart skips a beat and I feel like everything is perfect. Never in a million years did I imagine that the last two days would have happened to us.

It's tragic what happened to Riley and Charlie, but if not for them Chloe would not have been brought back into my life.

No fucking joke, it's true when they say everything happens for a reason.

Chloe has been a huge part of my life for years.

One day I'll marry that girl and forever she'll have my heart.

When I tell her my vows, it's not just words that will be said.

She'll understand exactly what I mean when I tell her…

You are my soul mate.

You are the love of my life.

You Chloe are my forever. I've been touched by you and only you.

Epilogue
Five Months Later
September 2013

I guess people are right when they say, you don't really know what you've got till it's gone.

That is exactly what happened to me a little over nine months ago.

I never would have thought that things would have come around full circle for us, but thankfully Derrick and I have a love that is stronger than anything. Really we are indestructible. I don't know how I got so lucky to have him in my life. In fact, at times, I don't know why he put up with my shit for so many years. But something about him was drawn to me. No matter what happened or what I did to hurt him or those that we loved, Derrick always stuck by my side.

When I made that promise to myself five months ago, I never intended for things to go my way. I was dead set on making sure that I was the servant to my boyfriend and our families, but in turn they rewarded me with so much.

Some days are harder than others. I still have to take a step back, evaluate the things that I have and be grateful more than anything. I can't take things or my loved ones for granted anymore.

I made a pact with myself to live everyday to the fullest. To always think of others before I think of myself. It's not always easy, but I've made a lot of progress.

It isn't easy to go from a heartless bitch to a caring saint over night, but I'm doing my best and that is all I can ask myself for each day.

But today, yes today is the day I've waited a long time for. It's time for Derrick and me to take this next step. After all he's done for me. I need to do this for him.

He has no clue what is going to happen tonight, but I hope to hell I'm able to pull it off as planned.

I've been working for the Boston Red Sox as the field analyst for the past five months. I love everything about my job, the kneecap to kneecap coverage with the team and the fact that I can live in Boston close to my family. I truly have everything I've ever dreamed of right here in front of me and now, yes now I need to take matters into my own hands and take a huge step forward. I'm scared, hell yes I'm scared, but it's time to do this and I'm more than ready.

Looking around my office and at the clock on the wall, I realize that I only have an hour left to finish up this interview spotlight that I'm planning for next week. After this is wrapped up I'm off to go get Riley. I hope that everything is in order that I asked for so we don't have to spend so much time picking up last minute things.

My phone starts to buzz across my desk and see that Char is calling.

"Hey lady what's up?" I ask in a cheery tone.

I sure as hell appreciate my sister more than ever. After all I almost lost her this year.

"Hey Chloe, minor problem....but don't freak." She says with a giggle.

"Shit Char, you can't say that and expect me not to freak. What's wrong?" I say with a pout.

"Well I went to lunch with Derrick today, just like I was supposed to and he said he was going to work late tonight. He has that huge case coming up next week and if he nails this he gets senior partner."

"Shit! Damn it! Blah! Okay I'm not going to freak out. It will be okay, I'll just rearrange some things and it will still work out."

"Yes it will. You've got a great attitude Chloe. I must say I really like this new side of you. It's so much easier to get along with you now."

"Char, don't start. I'm trying my best to stay cool and calm."

"Okay, okay, I'm sorry. It's just such an exciting night and I want everything to be perfect."

"Yeah, Char you and me both. You don't think he has any idea of what I'm up to, do you?"

"Nah, he's so wrapped up in the case he doesn't even realize he put on two different shoes today."

"Shit, Char that isn't funny."

"Yeah he didn't think so either when I pointed it out to him at lunch."

"Okay well I have to go and finish up here. I'm still picking Riley up, right?"

"Yep! Okay Chloe relax, it will all be okay. I'm so excited I could scream."

"Yeah just not in my ear this time. Okay I'll see you later on, thanks for everything Char. Love ya."

"Love you too Chloe."

I hit the red end button on my phone and take a seat back at my desk. I can't imagine if that girl was not in my life. My sister and I have grown so close since the accident. She truly is my best friend and I would be lost without her.

A few days after the initial trauma of the accident we were all on pins and needles waiting for Char to wake the hell up. One night after everyone had gone home I decided to stay so Riley could get some sleep. The poor guy never left the hospital. The staff was nice enough to bring in an extra chair that extended out to a lounge like bed and let him shower in her bathroom. I really do admire the way he cares about her. They are both so lucky to have one another in their lives.

While sitting back in Riley's chair I saw a movement out of the corner of my eye. Thinking it was just my imagination playing tricks on me I went back to doing some work on my iPad. A few minutes later the monitors started to beep and I stood up next to Char. Holding her hand I caressed her palm and started talking to her.

Within a few moments the nurse walked in to check on Char's vitals. I continued to watch her as her eyelids started to flutter and a cough escaped her throat. I knew at any moment something big was going to happen and I was right.

Char's beautiful big brown eyes opened and she watched the nurse and me as she tried to focus. It took her a bit till she was able to open them fully, but when she did I felt the tears begin to fall down my cheeks.

I quickly grabbed my phone and dialed Riley's number. Once he answered, I told him to call Mom, Dad and Derrick to get down here quick.

Ever since that day I swore to myself that I would never disappoint or hurt my sister again. We're closer than ever and spend as much time together as possible. In fact if one of us is not at the other's house we're out doing girl stuff while the boys are watching a game or at the pub. Life with us is just perfect and I wouldn't change a thing.

I glance over at the time on my computer screen, "shit!" I shout. I need to finish this up later, it's time to get out of here and go get Riley. Pulling together all the papers on my desk and shutting down my laptop, I then lock up and make my way to my car.

I pull into Taylor & Sons Contracting and Riley is already out standing by his Durango. As I slide my car in next to his, he stands there shaking his head at me. I let out a giggle and know that he's going to give me shit for being late.

He hops in the car and leans over to give me a hug.

"Thanks so much for doing all this with me. I know Char has her hands full keeping Derrick busy, well at least she was supposed to be. Now he has to work late so we're going to have to skip the game and go right into stage two of the night."

"Fuck Chloe calm down, you're talking to me like you're on speed or something…wait did you take drugs before you came and got me. You know how I hate that shit."

I smack his arm and put the car in reverse.

"Shut the hell up Riley, my nerves are shot to hell. I don't want to blow this tonight. It means a lot to me that everything goes perfect."

"Everything will be fine don't worry, but I do have one question. How are you getting him there since he won't be at the pub to watch the game?"

"Well since he's going to be working late I thought I would text him to come get me at the stadium. I'll just tell him to come in and get me while I finish up some work. He loves walking around and being nosey, so I should be fine."

Riley and I spend the next hour getting everything from their house to the stadium. Thankfully the Red Sox are away today and since I am part of the team they granted me access to the field…an awesome perk I think.

It's 9:30 and go time. Derrick should be here any minute now. My nerves are killing me and my stomach is in knots. I walk out the stadium and glance around the field. The lights are lit and the set up in the outfield looks amazing. I'm so blessed to have so many people in my life to help me with this special night.

I walk out to the pitcher's mound and wait for him. I can feel my heart beating a mile a minute and I'm afraid I'm going to puke at any given moment. Tonight will change things for us and I can't wait to share this moment with him.

In the distance I can see him walking along the concourse and see him stop.

Why the hell is he stopping…don't stop, keep walking. He starts to move again and my heart begins to beat out a steady rhythm.

He starts to walk down the stairs and I can barely make out the expression on his face.

As he continues to walk closer and closer to me I can see his baby blues sparkle from the lights of the stadium. A smile is spread across his face and he reaches his hands out to me as he approaches.

He looks handsome wearing his dress pants, white button down shirt and green tie.

My lips lift in to a smile as he grabs me into his arms. He gives me a kiss on the lips and pulls me in closer to him. I can feel his heart beating and our souls instantly begin to communicate. His touch gives my body a warmth that only he can provide and it makes me feel so loved.

We pull away from our embrace and he looks into my eyes.

"I'm sorry I missed watching the game with you guys tonight, but glad I'm here with you now. What's going on here tonight anyway?" He asks looking behind me at the white tent set up in the outfield.

"Just follow me. I have something special planned for us tonight."

I take his hand in mine and start walking our way over to the white tent.

Once we're inside I'm instantly taken back to that night. Riley, Char and our parents did an amazing job setting everything up like I asked. There's a table set for two in the far corner and a wooden dance floor in the middle. Soft music is playing in the background and our dinner is set on the table waiting for us.

I look over at Derrick and the expression on his face is like nothing I've seen before.

"Chloe, this is amazing. You did this for us? How did you do this? I mean wow!" He says looking around the inside of the tent.

"Well actually I had a lot of help, but yeah this is all for us. I wanted tonight to be special for us. We have a lot to celebrate Derrick."

He looks at me and smiles. I love his smile. In fact I love everything about this man.

"Let's take a seat and eat. I know it's late, but I'm sure you're hungry."

"I'm starving."

We sit down and he takes the dome lids off our dinner plates. It's so late and I'm starved from not eating all day. Now that we're here, my nerves are a bit more at ease and feel like I could eat everything on my plate.

Dinner is absolutely amazing and we both clear our plates. I see Derrick glance around the room and I can hear our song start to play. He gets up from the table and extends his hand out to me.

"My I have this dance?" He asks.

"Of course, I was hoping you would ask." I reply with a flirtatious wink.

He walks me over to the small wooden dance floor area and swings me around into his arms. As we dance to our song, Lucky by Jason Mraz and Colbie Caillat, I envision what it will be like to dance with him to this song on our wedding day. He pulls me in closer to his warm body so that I can feel his heart beating against mine. This night is absolutely perfect and there's just one more thing I need to do.

I pull away from him just enough so that I can look into his eyes again.

"You're so good to me." I tell him and kiss his lips ever so softly. "I love you so much Derrick. No matter what we've been through we always make it work. You make us work. I love you."

"I love you too Chloe."

"Derrick you're the one constant thing in my life. Through everything we've been through the past nine years you always knew we would make it work. I don't know that I could be where I am without you. I thank god everyday that you stuck with me. You really are my world."

I hear the song start to play and my hands start to shake. With the melody of Marry Me by Train playing through the speakers I take Derrick's hands in mine.

"Derrick I can't tell you enough how special you are to me, or how much I love you. For the past nine years you've been my soul mate, the one I find peace with. You're my forever Derrick and today is just the beginning of great things to come for us. Without you in my life things would be empty. You honestly make me who I am. I'm a better woman now because of you. I don't want to spend another day of my life without you by my side. I know what I'm about to do is not the customary thing to do, but for us I feel it's perfect."

I take a step back from him and get down on one knee. I look up at his tall frame and a smile crosses his face. He steps back and kneels down in front of me. Our hands are interlocked and he kisses me on the lips.

"I love you with all that I am Derrick Mason Peters, will you marry me?"

He looks at me, the smile never falling from his face.

"Chloe you make me the happiest I've ever been. Without you, I feel like a huge part of my life is missing something. I would love to marry you, but we need to do this the right way."

He helps me stand so that we're still facing one another.

A gasp escapes me as he reaches into his pocket and kneels back down in front of me.

"Chloe, I've carried this around with me since the day you moved back into our home. I've known my entire life that you would be my wife. I kept waiting for the perfect moment to ask you to marry me and I think I've found it."

The tears begin to fall from my cheeks and I bend down to kiss him.

"Chloe will you marry me, be my soul mate for eternity and always stay by my side?"

I nod my head up and down a million times while shouting yes.

Derrick stands and pulls me into him.

"I want to hear you say it Angel."

I smile at him and say, "Of course I'll marry you Derrick, you're it for me and we're going to have a beautiful future together. I've been touched by you."

Touched By You Playlist

A Thousand Years by Christina Perri

Just Give Me A Reason by P!nk featuring Nate Ruess

Need You Know by Lady Antebellum

U Got It Bad by Usher

Heaven Sent by Keisha Cole

True Love by P!nk featuring Lily Allen

Not Over You by Gavin DeGraw

Marry Me by Train

Talking To The Moon by Bruno Mars

Lucky by Jason Mraz featuring Colbie Caillat

Publishing Schedule

Touch Me August 31, 2013

Touched By You October 31, 2013

Touched By Another December 31, 2013

You've Been Touched January 31, 2014

Pierced Love November 30, 2013

The Cursed Series Spring 2014

About the Author

t. h.snyder is my pen name.

I am a 34 year old wife of ten years and mother to our two amazing kids.

I became an avid reader in spring of 2012 and since have read over 250 books.

My genre of interest ranges from Romance to thrilling Paranormal.

This is more than just a hobby for me, it's a passion to read the words of great authors and bring life to their stories with my reviews and character castings.

I started writing my first novel in June of 2013 and I am anxious to see where this journey takes me!!

You can continue to show your support by liking and following me on Facebook, Twitter, and Goodreads.

https://www.facebook.com/pages/Author-t-h-snyder/1391579264389587

https://twitter.com/thsnyder4

http://www.goodreads.com/book/show/18136883-touch-me

Made in the USA
Charleston, SC
18 November 2013